Coming Out in Ten Dates

A Later in Life Lesbian Romantic Comedy

by

Reba Bale

Table of Contents

Chapter One: The Challenge..1

Chapter Two: Shopping for Lesbians 5

Chapter Three: Getting Grilled...8

Chapter Four: The First Kiss...12

Chapter Five: The Coffee Date...16

Chapter Six: The Meet Cute...20

Chapter Seven: The Dance...25

Chapter Eight: Weird Food...29

Chapter Nine: Facing the Firing Squad................................33

Chapter Ten: Necking Like Teenagers..................................37

Chapter Eleven: Popping That Cherry 40

Chapter Twelve: The Post-Game Report................................45

Chapter Thirteen: The Double Date......................................49

Chapter Fourteen: Ghosted..54

Chapter Fifteen: 3 Dates in 3 Days...58

Chapter Sixteen: This Date Doesn't Count............................63

Chapter Seventeen: Just Passing Through..............................67

Chapter Eighteen: Kissing My Friend....................................71

Chapter Nineteen: Was It Something I Said? 75

Chapter Twenty: Second Chances 78

Chapter Twenty-One: We Had "The Night" 82

Chapter Twenty-Two: The Third Date...................................86

Chapter Twenty-Three: Feels Like Making Love....................90

Chapter Twenty-Four: Making It Official...............................94

Chapter Twenty-Five: The Happily Ever After 99

The Divorcee's First Time | A Contemporary Lesbian Romance 104

You'll be the first to hear about new releases, special sales, and free offers. 110

Copyright

---

1.   https://paperorpixels.com/

About This Book

Who knew coming out as a lesbian in midlife would be such a challenge?

After eighteen years of marriage, Rebecca finally admits the truth: she likes women. Tired of living a lie, she divorces her befuddled husband and sets out to explore life as a newly single lesbian woman.

Concerned that Rebecca will fall for the first sweet-talking sapphic sister she meets, her sister Alice challenges Rebecca to go on ten dates with ten different women to explore Seattle's lesbian dating scene. And she's recruited all of her friends to try to fix Rebecca up!

Little did she know dating women would be such an adventure...good dates, bad dates, totally weird dates...Rebecca is going to experience them all before she finally pops her lesbian cherry and finds "the one".

"Coming Out in Ten Dates" is a later in life romantic comedy set in the "Friends to Lovers" world. If you like steamy but sweet romances with a lot of snark and a heart-warming happily ever after, check out this fun lesbian romance today.

Author's Note: This story was previously published in serial format as "Coming Out in Ten Dates" episodes 1-25. The story has been expanded from its original format.

Be sure to check out a free preview of Reba Bale's lesbian romance "The Divorcee's First Time" at the end of this book!

Dedication

For everyone who found the courage to leave their old life behind and seek out new adventures. And for all the bad dates I found on dating apps – you are all my inspiration because if I didn't laugh, I'd cry.

Join My Newsletter

Want a free book? Join my newsletter and you'll receive a fun subscriber gift. I promise I will only email you when there are new releases or special sales, usually twice a month.

Visit my newsletter sign-up page at bit.ly/RebaBaleSapphic[2] to join today.

Chapter One: The Challenge

"I told Rob I wanted a divorce."

My sister choked on her coffee, sending a spray of droplets onto the table between us.

"Jeez Alice, be careful."

"Warn a girl if you're going to drop news like that," Alice chided, dabbing at the table with a napkin. "You're getting a divorce? I don't understand. You guys have been together since you were eighteen. I thought you were happy."

I placed an elbow on the table and rested my chin in my palm. "I love Rob. He's my best friend and I'll always love him. But I'm not in love with him, Alice. I don't think I ever was."

"You have two kids together," she reminded me, as if I could forget my two awesome kids. "I mean, you and Rob were always everyone's 'life goals' couple, the ones who made it for eighteen years. I figured you'd die together side by side in your rockers at the old folks' home."

"Well, clearly you've given my death a lot of thought, but that's not how I want my life to go. Not anymore."

"What did he do to you?" My sister's voice hardened.

"Rob? Nothing."

"Is he cheating on you? Did he hit you? Gamble away your retirement?"

Alice's hands balled into fists, her face starting to turn red.

"No, no, nothing like that," I told her.

"Oh my God! Are you having an affair?" Alice looked shocked and scintillated.

"No, of course not."

"Then why the divorce?"

"I'm a lesbian."

Alice's mouth dropped open. This was news to my sister, probably because she'd come out to our family way back when we were in high school, and I'd never mentioned anything about me also liking women.

"How are you a lesbian?" she frowned.

"The usual way, I suspect."

"Wait, start at the beginning. I'm confused."

"I've been with Rob for twenty years and he's never given me an orgasm."

A woman at the next table looked over at me disapprovingly. I frowned right back. There were no children in the vicinity.

"You're divorcing him because he's never given you an orgasm?" my sister clarified. "That doesn't mean you're a lesbian."

"I'm aware of that," I said impatiently. "I was at the gym one day, reading a lesbian romance book while I rode the recumbent bike, and I was surrounded by all these women of different shapes and sizes working out. A couple of them excited me more than I ever remember feeling when I saw my husband. I found myself wishing I could go up to one of them and ask them out."

"And did you?"

I shook my head. "No, but I went home and got myself off in the tub with the detachable shower head. I was laying there in the tub, still trembling from my orgasm, and I realized that whenever I masturbate, I imagine women. Or having a threesome with another couple."

"So you're telling me that not only are you a lesbian, but you want a threesome too?"

"I wouldn't say no."

My sister sipped her coffee for a full two minutes, possibly the longest amount of time she'd spent in silence since she learned to talk thirty-three years ago. While she was lost in thought, I studied her, noting how similar we were despite our three year age difference.

We both had shoulder-length brown hair. Mine was naturally straighter while Alice's was wavy unless she straightened it. With our matching brown eyes, creamy complexions, and similar builds, there was no mistaking that we were sisters.

"How did it go with Rob?" she finally asked.

"He was surprised. Sad. Also a little hurt of course. I'm not sure he believes that I wasn't lying to him all these years, I just figured this out myself," I explained. "He suggested that we separate for a while and I 'try' being a lesbian, but I told him we needed a clean break."

"Wow, okay."

I cleared my throat. "I was hoping that you and Jewel could show me the ropes of being a lesbian," I said, referring to Alice's wife.

"You want to sleep with us?" she asked in shock.

The woman at the next table jumped out of her chair like she'd been shocked, storming away.

"Oh my God!" I said in horror. "What the hell? I meant, I was hoping you could help me meet some women or figure out how to meet them. I haven't dated since I was in high school. I don't even know how it works now. Like do I sign up for Tinder or something?"

"No way. We'll help you, but I have one condition. Think of it as a challenge, really."

"What?"

"We have a joke in the lesbian community: what does a lesbian bring on a second date? A U-Haul."

My sister grinned as she took another sip of her drink.

"I don't understand."

"Some lesbians tend to get attached very quickly. Not all of them, of course, but there's a segment of the population that gets very clingy very fast. Believe me, I've dated a lot of those women over the years."

Alice reached out to grab my hand, her brown eyes meeting mine.

"Rob was your first steady boyfriend, Rebecca, so you've never learned how to date. If you're going to do this, you need some time to find yourself, to figure out who you are as a lesbian, and as a grown-up entering the dating world for the first time in twenty years."

"So, what's the challenge, exactly?"

"Promise me that you'll go on ten first dates before you take any second dates. Spend time with ten different women and then if you like any of them, you can go back for seconds after the ten dates are complete."

"Can I have sex with any of them?" I asked. "Because it's been a long time. A very, very long time."

The sexual part of my relationship had died years ago. We didn't even bother on birthdays anymore. In fact, I couldn't even remember how long it had been since I'd had sex, that's how long it had been.

Alice held up her hand. "I don't need the gory details, big sister. You do whatever you want on your ten first dates, but under no circumstances should they last more than twenty-four hours. Do we have a deal?"

"If I agree, you'll help me find ten women to date at least once?"

"Yes."

"Okay, we have a deal."

Chapter Two: Shopping for Lesbians

"Thanks for letting me stay here."

I looked around the tiny studio apartment with a sense of satisfaction. For the first time in my life, I was going to be living on my own. Well, on my own in the basement apartment that my sister and her wife rented out on Airbnb. Fortunately, they'd just remodeled it, so it wasn't rented to anyone else for the foreseeable future.

"We're glad to have you," Jewel said sweetly. "You can stay here as long as you want."

My sister-in-law was awesome. Even though she was seven years younger than Alice, she seemed to be the more mature one in their relationship.

"Would you like to join us for dinner tonight?" Alice asked. "Jewel and I were planning to grill some food and eat outside."

It was a rare warm and sunny spring day in Seattle. Like every good Pacific Northwesterner, we wanted to take advantage of the good weather before we descended back into dreary rain for the next month.

"That sounds great, thanks, if it's not an imposition."

"It's not an imposition at all," Jewel told me. "We thought we could make your shopping list."

"I don't think I need anything," I replied, confused. "I brought some food over from my house. Well, Rob's house."

"Your dating shopping list," Jewel told me with a laugh. "We're going to make a list of all your desired qualities in a date and things that are dealbreakers. Then we'll put the call out to our network and start setting you up."

Jewel and Alice were part of a large group of friends, all lesbians, who got together at least once a month. I'd never actually met any of them but had heard a lot about them from my sister.

"That sounds great. Should I bring anything?"

I looked around at the mess of boxes surrounding me and hoped they'd say no. There was no way I could find anything if they wanted me to contribute.

"Just yourself. We'll eat at six."

After a few hours of unpacking and organizing, I took a quick shower and made my way to the back yard. Their bungalow had a large backyard with a high fence, perfect for hanging out with friends.

Alice was at the grill, a giant pair of barbeque tongs in her hand.

"Hey big sister, you're just in time. Jewel made us mojitos."

My sister-in-law set a large pitcher on the picnic table, then returned a few minutes later with glasses.

"Can I help?"

"Not your first night here," Jewel said. She poured the light green liquid into three martini glasses. "Have a mojito. The mint is fresh."

We chatted easily as Alice grilled sausage, burgers, and vegetables. I was fortunate that my sister and I had always had such a close relationship. I knew that wasn't true for everyone.

As soon as we'd finished eating, Jewel came out with a spiral notebook and a pen. "Okay, time to make the list."

She looked at me expectantly. "Let's start with physical attributes. What do you find attractive in a woman, and what's a turn-off?"

"Um? I don't know."

"Sure you do," Alice chimed in. "Close your eyes and tell us about women you've seen at the gym or whatever and found attractive. What did they look like?"

I shut my eyes and imagined that I was at the gym.

"There's a woman I like to watch when she's running on the treadmill," I admitted. "She's kind of hot."

"Describe her," Alice ordered.

"She's got short white blonde hair, in one of those pixie cuts. Blue eyes that are really intense. She's tall and curvy. Not fat, just...womanly

I guess. And she has big boobs, big enough that she doubles up on her sports bras."

"Blonde. Short hair. Curvy. Big boobs. Athletic. Okay, got it," Jewel said as she scribbled on the pad of paper. "Now think of someone else."

I gave them a few descriptions, then Alice went inside the house and returned with several copies of "Us" magazine.

"Us magazine? Really?" I teased. "That's your idea of reading?"

"It's brain candy," Alice defended. "Now flip through the pictures and pretend like every celebrity in here is a lesbian. Pick a couple out like they're in a catalog."

I gave her a wry look but followed her instructions. After a while, a picture of what type of woman I found attractive emerged.

"Too bad I can't really order someone from a catalog," I joked. "It would probably be easier."

"Well, there is this lesbian dating app that some of our friends have used," Jewel said thoughtfully. "But first let's see if we have any good prospects from our circle of friends. Then you won't be starting with random strangers."

"Unless you're Madison and Camille," Alice laughed.

At my confused look she added, "My boss and friend Madison was crushing on this woman Camille, and Camille had the hots for her too. But they were too afraid to act on it because they're very different. So each of them signed up for the new lesbian dating app and they were matched with each other!"

"Wow, that's a weird coincidence."

"If it's meant to be, it's meant to be," Alice said softly, sending a look towards Jewel that was so loving it made my chest hurt.

That's what I wanted. That's what had been missing in my life. That kind of love. That kind of all-encompassing passion. I wanted it for myself. And if I had to date women I picked out of a catalog to do it, then that's what I was going to do.

Chapter Three: Getting Grilled

"Are you sure your friends won't mind me coming along?" I fretted.

I smoothed down my floral knee-length skirt, hoping it was appropriate for the Easter brunch with a new group of people. I'd lost a bit of weight since I'd asked for a divorce, but I still was curvy enough that sometimes I felt a bit frumpy.

"Madison's brunch parties are famous, and everyone is welcome," Alice assured me.

Her good friend and boss Madison was a billionaire tech guru, not that you'd know it by meeting her. She was totally down to Earth and super sweet. She lived in a large townhouse in Belltown, not the mansion you'd expect, with her partner Camille.

I trailed behind Alice and Jewel as they walked into the townhouse. Conversation stopped as ten sets of eyes turned our way.

"Alice! Jewel! Alice's sister I don't know! Welcome!" The young woman walked over to greet us, her hand extended. "Hi, I'm Camille. Welcome to our home."

"Hi Camille. I'm Rebecca. Thanks for having me here."

Camille's partner Madison came to give me a hug. "Rebecca, it's been a while. Nice to see you again. Let me introduce you to everyone, and then we can eat."

Everyone there was coupled up except for me, but it still felt very comfortable. It was interesting to meet the five couples who were there for brunch. They were all very different, ranging in ages from mid-twenties to early forties, but everyone there obviously in love.

I loaded up my plate with ham, eggs, hash browns, fruit, and scones, then joined my sister and Jewel on one of the couches. Everyone settled in the living room to eat, some pulling up dining room chairs. A tuxedoed waiter walked around taking plates, filling up coffee cups, and bringing fresh mimosas. It had been a while since I'd had the orange juice and champagne mixture, and I'd forgotten how much I liked it.

"So, Rebecca, not to put you on the spot or anything, but I understand you recently came out," a kind looking woman named Elizabeth said. "You should come see me for a tarot card reading sometime. We'll see what's in the cards for you."

"That sounds fun, thanks," I responded. "I'm trying to figure out who I am, if that makes sense. I was with the same guy since high school, married to him for eighteen years, and now suddenly I'm putting myself into the dating pool, and it's a different pool than I was in before."

"I love baby lesbians," a woman named Toya said. She was a lovely black woman with curly hair and a wide smile. "So fresh and eager."

Her partner Elana poked her in the side with an elbow. "Don't make her feel self-conscious."

"It's fine," I assured her. "I don't embarrass easily."

"As some of you know, I gave Rebecca a challenge," Alice announced. "I'm calling it my 'New Lesbian Challenge'. I may trademark it later. In fact, I think I'll write a book about it. I have a feeling it's a money maker."

We all chuckled. My little sister was always just a little bit over the top.

"What's the challenge?" Christine asked, looking at me.

"I need to go on ten different dates with ten different women before I accept any second dates," I explained.

"No dates over twenty-four hours," Alice reminded me. "That gives you time for sex but no marathon weekends where someone comes to spend the night and ends up staying for weeks."

"That makes sense," someone called from the buffet table.

"Have you been with a woman at all?" Elizabeth asked. "Or will one of these dates be popping your sapphic cherry?"

"Nope, I've never been with a woman. I've never been with anyone besides my husband. We lost our virginity together."

"But you've kissed a woman, right?" Elizabeth asked. "Like when you were drunk at a party in college or something?"

"No, not even then."

"I told you, she's always been a straight arrow," Alice piped up. "See what I did there?" she giggled.

I rolled my eyes.

"You're going to need to learn how to kiss a woman," Lila said. She looked vaguely familiar.

"I'm sorry, but have we met before?" I asked, trying to place her. "You look so familiar."

"It's because she's famous," Alice told me.

I frowned, studying the woman. When it was clear I wasn't putting the pieces together, Alice explained, "Lila is a famous singer. You've probably seen her on TV."

"Hmm, okay, that must be it." I glanced at Lila. "I mostly listen to eighties music, sorry."

"No problem. Sometimes it's nice to be anonymous."

I replayed Lila's words in my head.

"Wait, did you say I need to learn to kiss a woman?" I asked.

She nodded.

"Isn't it the same as kissing a man?"

"The same, but different," Lila said cryptically.

Her eyes lit up, and she looked at her partner Christine. "You know what I'm thinking, babe?"

Christine nodded. "Yeah, that's a good idea."

I'd always envied those couples who were so in tune they could sense each other's thoughts. My ex-husband and I were close friends, best friends even, but we'd never had that level of intimacy.

Lila turned back to me. "I'm about to star in my first movie."

"Congratulations."

"It's a lesbian space opera."

I nodded, even though I had no clue what that meant.

"My agent was saying that I need to get comfortable kissing women who aren't my partner," she explained. "It needs to look realistic for the cameras, but when I did my screen test, I got really nervous because it felt like I was cheating on Christine."

When I continued to stare at her blankly, Christine piped up.

"Lila needs to practice kissing women who aren't me, and you need to practice kissing women. You two should kiss each other."

"You want me to kiss your partner?" I asked in shock.

"Why not? It's just practice for both of you."

I looked around, wondering if I was being punked.

"Go on Rebecca," Alice shoved my shoulder. "Kiss the famous musician!"

Chapter Four: The First Kiss

"You want to kiss me?" I asked Lila. Now that I knew she was famous, I definitely recognized her. I'd seen her on one of those late night shows with one of the Jimmys.

"Or you can kiss me, I'm not particular."

She gave me a smile that I bet factored into a lot of people's fantasies. She was a beautiful woman.

I looked around, noting that every woman in the room was watching us avidly like we were some show streaming on Netflix.

"Um. I don't know."

"Come on," Alice prompted me. "You both need practice. It doesn't mean anything. That's an important lesson for the challenge, in fact. How to be with someone without catching feelings."

I glanced back at Susan. She gave me a nod.

"Seriously, it's okay."

She leaned over and whispered into Lila's ear loud enough for us to all hear, "I'll just spank you for it later."

Well, that was interesting. Which made me wonder, would I like to be spanked? I mean, Rob had never been into that kind of thing, but it sounded hot. Something for my list...

"Okay, let's do it," I said to Lila. "But not in front of all these people."

There was no way I wanted an audience for this. What if I messed something up?

Lila got up, dropping a kiss on top of her partner's head, and reached for my hand. "Let's go into the kitchen."

I followed Lila into the large, modern kitchen. Every surface was covered with dishes.

Lila looked around and shrugged. "Maybe let's try the laundry room."

We headed into the laundry room next to the kitchen, and Lila backed me up until my hips were pressed against the dryer.

"If you don't feel comfortable, we can stop at any time," Lila said, meeting my gaze. "It's just practice."

"Same for you," I replied.

Lila put her small hands on my shoulders, and my hands automatically moved to her hips. I licked my lips, and her gaze tracked my movement.

"The thing that's nice about kissing is lesbian is that there's no beard burn," she whispered. "Not usually anyway."

She leaned her head closer, until our lips were only a few inches apart.

"The best part of a first kiss is the lead-up."

I felt a weird tingle in my belly that I hadn't felt in years – excitement mixed with desire.

Lila moved closer and I giggled.

"What's so funny?" she asked.

"I was just thinking that if I told anyone that the first time I kissed a woman I was with a music superstar in a laundry room in some stranger's house, they would think I was crazy."

Lila smirked. "Just don't tell my agent. She would tell me to make you sign a non-disclosure agreement."

"I would never violate your privacy," I promised.

"Good."

Lila moved closer and pressed her lips against mine. They felt soft.

After a long moment, I felt her tongue peek out, sliding along the seam of my lips. I opened for her, and her tongue slid into the heat of my mouth, moving against mine.

Holy crap! I'm kissing a woman! I thought.

Then I shut off my mind and let myself just feel the kiss.

Lila pushed her fingers through my hair, tilting my head, and pressed her body against mine. I knew this was fake, I knew it was only for practice, yet I couldn't help the way my nipples hardened into painful points against my bra.

Lila was a good kisser, and my body was taking notice. Arousal roared to life in my body for the first time in forever.

I moved my hands around to get a grip on her ass, pulling her closer still, thrilling at the feeling of touching someone soft and feminine, just like I'd dreamed about for years.

In that moment, I realized I'd been living a lie for way too long. Even in our earliest, most passionate days, my husband hadn't gotten me this wet with just a kiss. My panties were already damp, and I couldn't resist rolling my hips against Lila's.

When she finally pulled back, we were both breathless.

"How was it?" she whispered.

"Better than I could have ever imagined," I told her. "I'm definitely a lesbian."

"Well, you could be bi," she pointed out, stepping back.

I shook my head.

"No, definitely not bi."

"Well, that's good to know then," Lila straightened her shirt.

I put my hand on her arm, suddenly self-conscious. "Um, was that okay?" I asked. "It's been a long time since I kissed someone new."

The look she gave me was kind, but there was a hint of amusement in her eyes.

"You're definitely a good kisser," she reassured me. "Just enough firmness, not slobbery, I'd definitely give you an A-minus."

"What would I need to do to get an A-plus?" I asked curiously.

"Be Christine."

My heart pinched at the look of love on her face.

"Well, thanks for helping me," I said.

"Thanks for helping me," she responded immediately. "My agent will be thrilled. Should we get back out there?"

"Yeah."

We walked through the kitchen and back towards the living room. All conversation ceased as soon as we entered the room.

"How was it?" Alice asked breathlessly. Was it weird that my sister was even more invested in this kiss than I was?

"Good," we both answered in unison.

Christine got up and stalked across the room, her expression intense. Lila met her halfway.

Without a word, Christina grabbed Lila's head, bringing her down for a long, scorching kiss that no one could help but watch. It was so raw, so passionate, so claiming.

They stepped apart and Christine grabbed Lila's hand, pulling her towards the door.

"We'll see you all later, thanks for Easter brunch."

I stood there in confusion as they practically ran out the door. Had I caused trouble for the couple? Christine had said it was okay to kiss Lila.

"That's just their dynamic," Alice said, coming to put her arm around my shoulder. "They're a little...intense sometimes. I promise you, everything is okay."

"Now how about you join us on the couch? We have a list of women for you to try."

Chapter Five: The Coffee Date

"What should I wear for a coffee date?"

Alice looked up from picking out some tomatoes. The two of us were doing our weekly grocery shopping together.

"You have a date?" She sounded surprised.

"Yep, date number one is on the calendar."

"Who is she?" my sister asked.

"Her name is Marci, she's a friend of Christine's."

"It was nice of Christine to fix you up after you kissed her woman."

Every head in the produce section snapped my way.

"It was a practice kiss, and we all agreed it was okay ahead of time," I reminded her, loud enough for the eavesdroppers to hear. But my explanation just got me more disapproving looks.

"So, what do you think? Jeans and a blouse?"

"Which blouse?" my sister asked me, looking at me critically.

"Have you seen that blue blouse with the tiny white daisies? I was thinking of that one."

"Oh yeah, that makes your tits look fabulous," she said. "Just make sure you wear a bra with good support so you can get those girls up high."

The disapproving looks shifted to my sister, and I repressed a grin.

"Come on, I need to get home and do laundry."

Two days later I was ready to go on my first official date as a lesbian. It felt weird at age thirty-eight to suddenly be experiencing all these firsts: my first kiss with a woman, my first date with a woman, and if I played my cards right, my first time having sex with a woman would be some time soon.

But first, coffee...

We'd decided to meet at Morning Jolt, the coffee shop where Camille worked part-time. Apparently she and Madison had met there when Madison came in for her daily coffee, and somehow Madison now owned the shop. I wasn't clear why.

I walked into the coffee shop five minutes early, but as soon as I opened the door, someone called out to me.

"Rebecca?"

I turned to see a tall woman with very short brown hair and a trim figure. She looked like she was in her late twenties and was reasonably attractive, but not 'take my breath away' attractive. But I well knew there was more to romance than just looks.

"Grace?"

"That's me."

To my surprise, Grace pulled me in for a hug. I wasn't much of a hugger, especially with total strangers, but I decided to go with it. I inhaled subtly, getting a whiff of something citrusy.

We pulled apart and went up to the counter to order coffee. Camille wasn't there, and I decided I was glad about that. I didn't want to feel like she was watching me. I was nervous enough.

After a brief scuffle over who was going to pay, I purchased a latte for me and a black coffee for Grace. We headed toward an open table in the corner. Grace leaned back in her chair, stretching her long legs into the aisle and gave me a once-over.

"What kind of work do you do, Rebecca?"

God, I hated small talk. Somehow I didn't realize that dating would involve small talk, I don't know why. Maybe because the last time I dated the small talk was about what bands we liked or who was the hardest teacher.

"I'm an accountant," I told her. "I work in the fiscal department at the city."

"You must make good money, being a government employee and all," Grace said confidently.

"Um, well, I do okay."

"And you have same sex health insurance benefits then. That's nice, especially if you're with someone uninsured."

It seemed like a weird thing to focus on, but okay.

"I think it's required now to provide same sex partnership benefits," I answered. "At least for most employers. What about you? What do you do?"

"I'm between jobs right now," she said, her tone lighter than I would have expected.

"Oh gosh, I'm sorry to hear that." I knew there were a lot of people who'd lost their jobs after the pandemic. "What kind of job are you looking for?"

"I'm not really a nine-to-five person," she answered. Or non-answered, as the case may be.

I frowned. "So you like to work the swing shift?"

Grace chuckled like I'd said something entertaining.

"I'm really not a 'job' person," she said, making air quotes with her fingers.

"You're not?"

"I guess I'm just looking for a sugar mama," she said with a wink. "Someone I can play housewife with. I love to clean and I'm a great cook."

"How do you know Christine again?" I asked, suddenly wondering why my sister's friend thought we'd be a good match. Maybe she was more upset about me kissing her partner than she'd let on.

"We used to be neighbors, before I got evicted," Grace said. "Stupid landlord got so cranky when I couldn't pay my rent. Anyway, I hadn't seen Christine in a few years but then we ran into each other at yoga class last week and she told me about you."

"Ah, okay."

We spent an uncomfortable hour playing at small talk. Grace did ninety-nine percent of the talking, mostly about herself. I'd never been so glad to finish up a coffee in my life. I might be a new lesbian, but I'd been around enough to spot someone who was a narcissist.

"You want another?" Grace asked, pointing to my empty cup.

"No thanks. This has been great, but I really need to go. I promised my sister I'd meet her to go shopping...for shoes."

I was a terrible liar, and from the look on Grace's face, she knew it.

"Oh, I see." Her voice turned cold. "Well, it's clear that neither of us is feeling this, so let's just call it a day."

Old Rebecca would have rushed to smooth her ruffled feelings, but New Rebecca didn't want to waste time with anyone who wasn't on the same page. I'd spent way too much time putting aside my wants and needs for others. This was my 'me time' and I meant to enjoy it.

After tossing our empty coffee cups, Grace and I headed outside into the grey drizzle. It suited my mood. I only hoped all my dates weren't going to be like this.

Chapter Six: The Meet Cute

"How was your coffee date?" Jewel asked later that day when I ran into her in the driveway. She looked so excited for me that I almost hated to burst her bubble.

"She's a total narcissist."

"Any sparks though?"

"None."

"Well, that sucks," Jewel said. "Do you have another one lined up yet?"

"Not yet."

"Well, I know the girls have some feelers out, so don't worry." Jewel gave me an encouraging smile.

"Oh, I'm not worried," I told her. "And I'm not in a rush to find a partner. Remember this is my first time living alone. I moved from my parents' house to living with my husband, and then we had kids right away. Honestly, I'm looking forward to spending some time on my own as much as I'm looking forward to doing some dating."

"I love that."

"In fact, I'm going to an art show tomorrow, all alone," I said proudly. To someone like Jewel who had traveled the world all alone, it probably seemed like nothing. But to me, it was huge.

"Have a great time."

The next day I wandered around the art gallery, checking out the exhibit of modern art by local artists. I found myself in a room full of metal sculptures and found myself drawn to the far end of the room. I studied the corner display, a large metal sculpture that almost looked like a flower. I was standing on my tiptoes, trying to see the top better, when I heard a voice behind me.

"Be careful."

I startled, lunging forward towards the sculpture. A pair of arms came around my waist, pulling me back and keeping me from knocking over the sculpture. I stood completely still for a moment, then pulled away, turning to face my rescuer with a hand over my rapidly beating heart.

"You scared me."

"You were getting too close to the sculpture," she rejoined. "That's why there's a velvet rope around it. So people don't touch it."

I didn't appreciate being chastised like a child by this woman. I looked her up and down. She had a bohemian kind of look, with a long broomstick skirt, boots, and a peasant top that did little to hide her ample breasts. Long black hair, streaked with grey, hung in waves around her shoulders. Her dark brown eyes were flashing at me in annoyance, her lips pressed into a thin line. She was beautiful.

"Well, thanks for the assist," I said, deciding not to argue.

For some reason, my gaze seemed fixed on her breasts. Wait, was I a breast woman now? I guess I did have that on the list we'd made.

"What do you think about the sculpture?" she asked curiously, drawing my attention back to her face.

"Eh. I guess it's okay."

"Just okay?" She seemed entertained by my answer.

"I mean, it's nice enough. But I'm not sensing any emotion in it. And I know this is a modern art exhibit, but I'm not even clear what this thing is supposed to be."

"It's a vagina," the woman said sharply. "See the clitoris at the top?"

I studied it for a moment. Now that I knew what it was, I could see it was clearly a stylized vagina, but I still didn't love it.

"Hmm. I thought it was some kind of fanciful flower."

"Some might say you're correct. The vagina is often compared to a flower."

"It's just not my cup of tea," I said. "I mean, why make a sculpture of a vagina hidden as a flower?"

"It's art," the woman chastised me, crossing her arms beneath her chest. The movement made her breasts rise even more. "Just like the body is art."

"It's weird."

I stepped over to look at the next piece of art, a sculpture that looked like some kind of bird. The woman followed me.

"Well, I'm sorry you don't like my work," she said archly. "I know it doesn't speak to everyone. Not everyone can appreciate my vision."

"This is yours?" I asked in surprise. "You're the artist?"

I guess I should have been embarrassed, but something about this woman was really annoying me. Or maybe it was attraction. She stood close to me, and I could feel the air practically vibrating between us.

"Yes, I am."

When I didn't say anything else, she gave me a long look. I licked my lips, growing uncomfortable under her perusal. And maybe the tiniest bit turned on. Her gaze sharpened on my lips.

"May I ask you a personal question?" It was phrased as a question, but the tone was more like an order.

"I guess so."

"You date women, correct?"

I wondered if there was some newly visible sign of my being a lesbian, like some kind of a sapphic bat signal, or if it was just a lucky guess.

"I'm trying to," I mumbled, mostly to myself.

"Can I buy you a drink?" she asked.

My head shot up in surprise.

"I told you I don't like your work and you want to buy me a drink?" I asked suspiciously. "Is this a ploy to get me to go with you somewhere so you can murder me for insulting your art?"

Her laugh was deep and throaty.

"Oh yes, I like you."

She grabbed my hand, and I felt a definite tingle. I suppressed a shiver.

"Come with me. There's a good bar up the street."

I followed her to a bar a couple blocks up. It looked like a neighborhood tavern, a battered sign proclaiming that it was called "Miller's." As the woman pushed the door open, I pulled her back onto the sidewalk.

"Wait, what's your name?" I asked.

"Veronica," she told me. "But my friends call me Ronnie. And you are?"

"Rebecca."

"Well Becca, come on in and have a drink while we get to know each other. I must confess that you fascinate me."

No one had ever called me Becca before, but I kind of liked it.

Miller's was a little dated, with a scarred bar top, mismatched furniture, and an ancient jukebox in the corner. I liked it immediately. I hated all the fancy frou-frou bars teeming with hipsters that were scattered around Seattle.

"Hey Big Bob," Veronica greeted the imposingly large man behind the bar. "We'll have a Jack and Coke and..."

She looked at me questioningly.

"That sounds good to me."

"Two Jack and Cokes please, Big Bob."

"You got it, Ronnie."

We headed towards one of the high-backed booths that ran along the wall, facing each other across the scuffed table. Big Bob brought us two drinks, and Veronica held hers up for a toast.

"To new friendships," she said. "And maybe more."

I clicked her glass with my own and took a sip of my drink. It was strong enough to make my eyes widen.

"Big Bob pours a good shot, especially if he knows you," Veronica said, reading my mind.

She leaned her elbows onto the table, putting her cleavage on display again. "Now Becca, I must hear everything about you."

Chapter Seven: The Dance

Two drinks and a couple of life stories later, I had to admit that I was enjoying my impromptu date with Veronica. She was a self-employed artist, about as far away from a government accountant as you could get, and yet we had a lot in common.

Plus, Veronica seemed fun and spontaneous, something I definitely needed in my life.

"Hey! Let's dance."

I looked at Veronica, then looked around at the mostly dead bar. "Dance where?"

"There's a jukebox," she said, as if that was the obvious answer. Hopping out of her side of the booth, she held out her hand. "Come on."

I followed her to the jukebox. After a quick perusal, she slid in a couple of quarters and made her selection. The bar was filled with the sounds of Wham's "Careless Whisper".

Veronica pulled me into her arms, hands at my waist, and I placed my hands on her shoulders. We swayed to the music for a while, gradually getting closer, until our bodies were pressed up against each other. We were almost the same height, and all of our other body parts lined up.

It was a weird sensation, dancing with my boobs pressed against another pair. But I liked it.

The song changed to Melissa Etheridge's "Suede". My entire body was humming, this close to Veronica. We were wrapped in our own little sensual bubble, pressed tightly together, our bodies in sync.

When the song wrapped up, we headed back to the table, but this time Veronica slid into the booth on the same side as me. As soon as we were seated in the booth, she turned to face me.

"I want to kiss you, Becca. If you don't want this, tell me to stop."

I licked my lips. "Kiss me."

She surged forward, her lips taking mine in a passionate kiss. I gripped Veronica's shoulders, holding her close. When Lila kissed me, I had let her take the lead, but with all the build-up with Veronica, I felt much more confident, giving as much as I took.

We kissed for a long time, hands roving, teeth clashing, until I was more hot and bothered than I'd been in maybe forever.

Veronica met my gaze. "I live just up the street."

She didn't need to ask me twice. "Let's go."

We paid the bill and walked hand in hand to Veronica's apartment a few blocks away. We made it halfway up the stairs before we stopped to kiss again. A few minutes later, we practically fell into Veronica's apartment.

"I want you," Veronica whispered as she pressed me against the door.

"I've never done this before," I told her reluctantly.

"Done what?" she asked in confusion.

"Slept with a woman."

She took a step back. "Wow, you said that you had newly come out, but I figured you'd been sleeping around, making up for lost time."

I shook my head. "My sister made me promise that I'd go on ten first dates with ten different women before I got serious about anyone or went on a second date."

"You don't have to be serious about someone to have sex, Becca."

"Yeah, I know."

We looked at each other, not speaking, and I chastised myself for speaking up. Veronica's face had changed, the look of lust replaced with caution.

"I'm sorry, I guess I shouldn't have said anything about this being my first time, but it felt dishonest not to mention it."

Veronica moved closer, her hands coming to my hips, and I met her dark gaze.

"Here's the thing Becca, I like you. I like you a lot. But I've been hurt by newbies before and, well it's a lot of responsibility guiding someone through their first time. It's more of a girlfriend thing than a casual hook-up thing."

"Sure, I get it. I'll go."

She squeezed my hips. "I don't want you to go. I'm going to get you off, and then when you're done with your ten dates, I want you to call me."

My panties flooded at the getting off part, but still...

"Get me off? I mean, what about you?"

She smiled. "This will bring both of us pleasure, don't worry. Sit on the couch."

I settled in the middle of the red velvet couch, and Veronica kneeled in front of me, looking up at me from beneath her eyelashes. "Lean back."

She shifted me until I was laying sideways on the couch, a pillow beneath my head, then shoved my skirt up to my waist.

Her hands ran lightly up my legs and the outside of my hips before coming to the waistband of my sensible cotton underwear. With a smile, she pulled them down, tossing them behind her, leaving me bare.

Veronica studied my pussy until I began to squirm from the perusal. I wondered if I should start waxing or something. I mean, I kept things clean down there, but I knew a lot of women waxed these days.

"Beautiful," she breathed.

She lowered her head and gave me a long swipe on the external surface of my pussy lips. I jumped like I'd been shocked.

"Relax, baby."

Moving my thighs to her shoulders, Veronica settled on her belly on the couch, her face right up against my pussy. Using her fingers to spread me wide, she lapped up my essence like it was the best thing she'd ever tasted.

Up and down, up and down, from bottom to top, she licked my pussy, until I was a quivering mess.

My ex-husband had never been a big fan of going down on me, generally saving it for special occasions. The difference between someone eating you out from a sense of obligation compared to someone who actually liked it was appreciable.

Veronica slid a finger into my channel and began pumping in and out, while focusing her tongue around my clit, circling it but never getting exactly where I needed her. My hips moved, circled, desperate to get her where I needed her.

"I need..." My voice came out like a whine.

"I know what you need, greedy girl."

Veronica's voice held a hint of laughter.

"Don't worry, I've got you, just let go."

She added a second finger to my channel, pumping in and out roughly, then licked her way slowly up and around my clit. Just when I was least expecting it, she sucked my clit into her mouth and bit down lightly with her teeth.

"Oh God!"

That was all I got out before I was flying, my orgasm crashing through me like a freaking tsunami. I was bucking beneath Veronica, my head whipping from side to side as I rode out the waves, whimpering in pleasure.

She stroked me gently as I finally came down from the intense orgasm. When Veronica lifted her head, I could see she was wet with my juices. I sat up, giving her a deep kiss, turned on by tasting myself on her.

"That was...wow, thank you."

"Believe me Becca, it was my pleasure."

She pushed to her feet and extended a hand.

"Now get out of here before I change my mind and keep you here forever."

Chapter Eight: Weird Food

Ever since Veronica had eaten me out, I couldn't get her off my mind. I'd spent two straight nights fantasizing about her with my vibrator in hand.

"I want to call her," I whined to my sister Alice a few days later. "I really like her."

"See? This is exactly why I gave you the Ten Date Challenge," she said. "You have absolutely no experience dating – men or women. You are the dating equivalent of a fourteen year old girl right now, Rebecca. You have to learn not to fall in love with every person who knows how to use their tongue."

"Alice!" I laughed.

"Besides, I have someone new for you to meet. It's someone that I work with, but we're not in the same department or anything, so it won't be weird if you hate each other." She handed me a slip of paper. "Her name is Amber, she's expecting your call."

After chatting on the phone for a while, Amber and I agreed to meet for lunch the following Saturday.

"Pick a place you like," Amber said. "I'll meet you there."

We met at a nearby McTarnahan's, a local brewery chain that had made a name for itself by buying up old schools and factories and turning them into restaurants and hotels. A friend had told me that she always met her blind dates at this McTarnahan's location, partly because she liked their tater tots and partly because they had free parking. In Seattle, that was a bonus.

Amber met me by the front door, standing under an old sign that said, "Mrs. Basil's School for Wayward Girls". It felt appropriate.

"Hey Rebecca, nice to meet you," she said, giving me her hand. Her handshake was firm, not one of those limp fish handshakes so many women gave.

As we shook, I checked her out. She was a little bit younger than me, probably in her early thirties, and pretty tall for a woman, probably over six feet, and a little overweight. She had straight, shoulder length brown hair streaked with lines of purple, tiny round glasses, and she was wearing a Dr. Who tee shirt and form-fitting jeans. She definitely had a "nerd girl" thing going for her.

We headed into the building, looking for the main restaurant that was located in the converted school cafeteria. After getting shown to our seats, we started with the obligatory 'get to know you' questions.

I found out that Amber worked in IT, no surprise there, and had been single for about a year.

"I'm a serial monogamist," she explained. "I usually date someone for about a year, but then inevitably the woman wants to take the next step and I'm not ready. What about you? Are you a serial monogamist or do you like to play the field?"

"I don't know," I admitted. "I just accepted I was a lesbian a few months ago. Before that I was married to the same man for eighteen years. He was my high school sweetheart, so I haven't done much dating. Well, any dating, really."

Her eyes widened. "Wow, so this is all new to you?"

"Yeah."

"Well, congratulations on finally accepting your true self. It seems like a lot of women come out once they hit middle age."

Ouch, I thought. I didn't think I was middle aged. Not yet anyway. I wasn't even forty for cripe's sake.

We moved on to other subjects until the food came. Amber had ordered one of the burgers on the menu and I'd ordered a hummus platter that came with hummus, olives, feta cheese, vegetables, and bread.

I scooped some hummus onto a piece of pita bread and added a tomato to the top when I looked up to see Amber staring at me in disgust.

"What's the matter?" I asked, examining my food in case there was a bug in it or something.

"What is that?" she asked, her voice turning a little high-pitched.

I nodded at the food in my hand. "You mean the hummus?"

"Is that what the brown stuff is?" Her tone implied that I had a scoop of shit on my pita bread.

"Yeah, it's hummus, you haven't had it before?"

When she shook her hand, I slid my plate in her direction. "It's really good, garbanzo beans mixed with tahini and lemon. Try it."

She shook her head almost violently, her face reminiscent of my kids when they were toddlers and I tried to get them to eat vegetables.

"I don't eat weird food," she said adamantly.

Yep, same as a toddler.

"Hummus is a pretty common food," I said mildly. "It's a staple in many cultures, and a good source of protein."

"You can keep your brown stuff to yourself," she told me as she took a giant bite of her bacon cheeseburger. I resisted pointing out that her bacon and burger were also brown.

As I ate my hummus platter, which was delicious thank you very much, I pondered whether I would do a second date with someone who had such a weird reaction to food. I imagined bringing her to my mother's for Christmas and Amber telling my mother that one of her traditional German holiday dishes was too "weird" to try.

I stiffened in alarm. Holy shit, I'd been separated from Rob for a month now and hadn't told my mother!

Usually, we spoke once or twice a week, but she'd just gotten back from a monthlong cruise to Alaska with my father a couple of days ago. If she talked to one of my kids – or God forbid, Rob – before I broke the news, I was going to be in deep shit with her.

I wasn't worried about coming out to my parents. They'd been super supportive when Alice had told them she was gay back when we were in high school. I knew my mother well enough to know that it was the divorce that was going to upset her.

While Amber and I finished our meals and walked out to our cars I was still spinning about dealing with my mother.

Amber leaned in to give me a hug goodbye, a wry look on her face.

"I'm not feeling any sparks," she said. "Are you?"

I appreciated her honesty. Shaking my head, I gave her a rueful smile.

"None at all, I'm sorry."

"At least we tried," she said cheerfully. "It was nice to meet you. See you around."

I got into my car and decided I'd better go face the firing squad. It was time to see my mother.

Chapter Nine: Facing the Firing Squad

My mom picked up the phone on the second ring when I called her from my car.

"Hey Mom, is it okay for me to come over? I've got something important that I need to talk to you about."

"Sure honey. Your father and I are finally up and around. We've been sleeping for the entire two days since we got back. Cruising was more exhausting than we expected."

I turned my car in the direction of the suburb where I'd grown up. Alice and I were lucky, we'd been raised by two parents who were happily married, owned their house, and while we'd never been swimming in money, we had a comfortable middle class lifestyle. We hadn't really wanted for anything, and when Alice came out to my parents, they'd accepted her without missing a beat.

I knew well that most people weren't as blessed as we had been.

Thanks to the relentless Seattle traffic, it took me almost an hour to get up to my parents' house. An hour where I practiced various ways I could break the news to my parents, but I couldn't find one I liked.

In the end, I went with the direct approach.

When I got there, I settled at the dining room table, the place where we always had our serious discussions. My mother bustled around pouring my father and I coffee and apologizing profusely for not having any "good snacks" to share.

"It's fine Mom, really. I just came from a lunch date."

I'd used the terminology on purpose but got no reaction. I took a deep breath.

"Something happened while you were gone...," I started.

My mother squealed.

"Oh my God, are you pregnant honey? I mean I know it's been a while for you, but parenting a newborn will come right back to you, I promise. Plus, you're healthy, you should be fine carrying to term."

I shuddered.

"I'm not pregnant, Mom."

Her face fell.

"Is one of the girls pregnant then? I mean, they're still young, but so were you. They'll be okay."

I ignored her and blurted out, "Rob and I are getting a divorce."

My father spoke up for the first time since we sat down.

"That bastard. What did he do? I'll kill him."

I appreciated his response, especially since he really liked my ex-husband. Rob was his fishing buddy, the son Dad had never had. They'd always been tight.

"Rob didn't do anything, Dad. I'm the one who asked for a divorce."

"What? Why on Earth would you do that, Rebecca Anne?" Mom demanded, her face already set in the judgmental lines I'd anticipated for this conversation.

"I'm not in love with Rob. I haven't been for a long time."

She waved her hand dismissively.

"Please," she sniffed. "You don't have to be in love to be married. You build a life with someone based on partnership and respect. That's all you can ask for."

It wasn't exactly a glowing endorsement of marriage.

"I want more, Mom."

"Oh my God, do Samantha and Skyler know?" she asked, referencing my daughters. "Those poor girls, they're going to be devastated, coming from a broken home!"

"They're both in college, Mom, they don't even live at my home, broken or otherwise."

My daughters and four friends had rented a house near campus where they lived year round. Other than stopping by to see their parents when they needed money or wanted to raid the cabinets for food, Rob and I rarely saw them.

"I can't believe you're shaming our family with a divorce."

I sighed.

"Mom, it's not nineteen fifty-four. There's no shame. Most marriages end in divorce these days."

Mom's eyes dampened in what I knew were fake tears. She'd always had a flair for the dramatic.

"You and Rob have been married for what? Eighteen years? You can't give up on each other now."

"I'm gay."

"What?"

Mom gave me a look I'd seen her give to people who were talking to themselves on the street. The look that said, 'You are insane and I'm worried about you'.

I met her eyes, then my father's.

"I'm a lesbian."

"This isn't how it works dear."

My mother's tone turned patronizing.

"You don't just wake up and decide you're a lesbian. Maybe you should have your sister explain it to you."

"I've already come out to Alice, and she supports me. In fact, I'm renting her basement apartment."

I didn't mention that she was also helping me find women to date. I didn't want to give my mother a stroke.

"You moved out already?" Mom asked in shock. "We've only been gone a month!"

"This has been coming for a long time, Mom."

"Were you always a lesbian?" Dad asked me quietly. As usual, I had absolutely no idea what he was thinking.

"I think so. Looking back, I've been attracted to women for as long as I can remember. I just told myself it was a harmless fantasy," I explained. "But I realized I was living a lie, and I wanted to live a more authentic life. I'm a lesbian."

"Maybe you and Rob can have one of those open marriages," Mom said hopefully. "Then you wouldn't have to get divorced. You could stay married and when you...felt the urge, you could seek companionship."

My mother was suggesting that I have an open marriage? I couldn't believe it. How did she even know about open marriages?

"That's not fair to me or to Rob. It's over between us. We've already filed a non-contest divorce and signed an agreement for him to buy me out of the house."

"What about your job?" she asked.

"What about it?"

"What if they find out you're a lesbian?"

"I'm not going to get fired for being a lesbian. It's against the law to do that in Washington, and besides, my workplace is very progressive."

"You and Rob should go to marriage counseling," she suggested. "Maybe this is all a misunderstanding."

"It's not a misunderstanding. I'm a lesbian and we're getting divorced. I just wanted you to hear it from me."

"Well, it sounds like you made your mind up," Mom sniffed. "But don't come crying to me when you realize that being out there dating isn't as much fun as it sounds."

Don't I know it, I thought wryly.

Fortunately, my next date went even better than I expected.

Chapter Ten: Necking Like Teenagers

I have to admit, I didn't have high hopes for my next first date.

I'd met Lisa through Toya, one of my sister's friends. Toya had insisted that Lisa and I would get along great, but when we chatted on the telephone, it soon was obvious we didn't have a lot in common. Our personalities couldn't be more different.

We disagreed on sports, politics, reading material, and, of all things, rain. Lisa hated rain, where as a native Washingtonian, I loved it. Our conversation had nearly ground to a halt when by chance we'd realized that we both liked superhero movies.

After some discussion, we discovered that we both wanted to see one of the newly released superhero movies that featured a strong female lead.

I was encouraged by finding some common ground, and I figured that a movie date would be good, because then I wouldn't have to talk to her if I disliked her in real life.

Lisa was thirty-eight, exactly the same age as me, with long red hair and a pale complexion. She had a splattering of freckles across her nose that made her look younger than the lines at the side of her emerald green eyes would suggest.

She was a solid size ten, not skinny, not fat, with breasts that were too large for her frame. Or most people's frames really. Lisa met me at the theater wearing a short skirt, combat boots, and a tank top with a men's plaid shirt over it. It was a strange outfit, maybe a little too young for her, but somehow she managed to pull it off.

I was immediately attracted to her physically. The minute she shook my hand, I wanted her. But her personality in real life was as abrasive as it had been on the phone, so I kind of hated myself for how attracted I was to her. I couldn't ever remember feeling such a strong attraction for someone who annoyed me.

We grabbed a small tub of popcorn to share and two sodas, both of us having agreed that that if things went well we would go out for dinner after the movie. The theater was surprisingly empty, and after a short discussion, we settled in the very back row. I preferred to sit in the middle, but acquiesced to her desire to sit farther back since Lisa said sitting too close gave her a migraine.

Sitting down, our knees brushed against each other, and I felt a tingle of excitement. When I kept my knee touching hers, Lisa pressed against it subtly.

The lights went down, and as the credits started, I felt Lisa place her hand on my thigh. It burned through my pants like a brand. Her thumb stroked back and forth, the tiny touch ramping me up.

I turned to look at her, and she turned at the same time, and suddenly, it was game on. She grabbed the back of my head, bringing me forward to meet her over the arm rest, and pressed her lips against mine.

Lisa was the third woman I'd kissed now, but this didn't feel like Lila or even Veronica. Her lips were firm and demanding as she bit my lower lip, silently demanding entrance. Our tongues tangled almost frantically, as each of us fought for control.

Now this was a first kiss. This was the first kiss by which I'd judge every other first kiss that came after, I was totally sure.

We finally broke apart to catch our breath, and Lisa pulled up the arm rest between us, allowing us to move closer without a barrier. She ran one arm over the back of my seat, the other coming to my shoulder, then leaned forward again. I met her in the middle.

This kiss was slower, calmer, but just as mind blowing.

We ran our hands over each other's back and shoulders, exploring, and then she tangled her fingers in my hair, tugging the strands. I angled my head to the side, trying to deepen the kiss even more.

And then I did something that I'd been dreaming about for...well as long as I could remember. I reached my hands out and touched another woman's breasts.

I'd touched my own boobs a million times of course, but I'd never laid so much as a finger on another pair.

Lisa's breasts felt different than my own. Her breasts were large and pendulous – definitely more than a handful—and they somehow felt a bit firmer than mine did. I cupped my hands around her, one hand on each breast, and gave them a gentle squeeze. Lisa moaned against my mouth, letting me know that she liked it.

I was in heaven. The sound made my already damp panties completely soaked. My pussy was clenching, desperate to get in on the action. Was it possible to have an orgasm just from fondling another person's breasts?

Emboldened, I shifted my hands so I was still touching Lisa's breasts but was in a position where I was able to snag her nipples in the crook between my thumb and my pointer finger. Her nipples grew hard as I pinched them between my fingers.

Meanwhile Lisa's hands moved down to my waist. She slipped them beneath my shirt and traced the muscles of my back. When her hands broached the waistband of my pants, and her talented fingers started caressing the top of my ass, I moaned loudly.

I forgot we were in public, forgot that someone could see us or hear us, and just leaned into the sensations.

After several minutes—or several hours, who knew?—she pulled back and gripped my shoulders, meeting my eyes. Even in the dim light of the theater I could see the desire on her face.

"Rebecca," she gasped. "I want to fuck you so bad right now."

I damn near died on the spot.

"How about we get out of here?" she suggested.

I didn't hesitate in asking the only question that came to mind.

"My place or yours?"

Chapter Eleven: Popping That Cherry

I followed Lisa to her house, parking a little ways up the street. I'd gotten a little nervous on the short drive, and had almost called my sister twice, hoping for moral support. But then I reminded myself I was an adult. I didn't need a pep talk from my baby sister.

Lisa lived in a little bungalow a few miles away from the theater. She met me at the door, her gaze focused and intense. She grabbed my shirt, using it to pull me into the house. The door slammed behind us as she led me to the bedroom without a word.

Her bedroom was a little stark, done mostly in whites, but the room was light and airy. We sat on the bed, and to her credit, Lisa realized that I was nervous.

"Hey," she said, touching my cheek. "We don't have to do this if you changed your mind."

Just the light touch of her fingers against my cheek was enough to firm my resolve.

"I want to do this. I just...well I'm hoping I'm not bad at it."

"Bad at it? What does that mean?" Her eyes widened in realization. "Are you saying that you haven't had sex before?"

"I've had sex with men. Well, one man."

"But no women?" She frowned, but she looked more confused than annoyed.

"No. Well, not exactly. A woman ate me out last week, but I've never...um, done anything else other than that one time."

I met her gaze.

"I only came out as a lesbian recently."

She nodded thoughtfully.

"Well normally I'm not into being someone's gay tutor, but I want you so fucking bad I'm going to make an exception to my rule."

I breathed out a sigh of relief, remembering how Veronica didn't want to do more with me once she learned that I was inexperienced.

I'd worried that every woman I hooked up with would have the same concerns. Surely I couldn't be the only woman who came out in midlife?

"I...I just don't want to be a disappointment," I admitted.

"Here's the thing Rebecca, you're already familiar with the equipment, right? Do what feels good when someone does it to you and you'll do just fine."

She gave me a smirk.

"Plus, I tend to be pretty vocal. I'll tell you what I like, and what I don't like. You do the same for me."

She leaned forward, giving me a kiss that was surprisingly sweet. Our lips were pressed against each other, her fingers still on my cheek, but we were otherwise not touching.

Then suddenly the kiss turned hot, and our hands were everywhere, touching and exploring each other wherever we could reach.

I shoved her plaid shirt off her shoulders, and she unbuttoned my shirt. When our mouths broke apart, I practically ripped Lisa's tank top over her head, then we both removed our bras, leaving us topless. I stared at her boobs like a kid staring at their favorite dessert.

And maybe this would be my new favorite dessert.

I caught the bottom of one of Lisa's heavy breasts in my hand, pushing it upwards, then wrapped my lips around her nipple. It was softer than I expected. I explored her nipple with my tongue, then gave it an experimental nip my teeth. I was rewarded with a soft moan.

Lisa sat still, allowing me to explore her breasts to my heart's content, fascinated as I watched my efforts bring her nipples to hard peaks. When she couldn't take it anymore, she pulled back, breathing heavily.

"Here's what we're going to do," she said. "You're going to take off your pants and I'm going to make you come."

I held up one finger.

"Alternate proposal: we could both take off our pants, and we could make each other come at the same time."

"I like the way you think, Rebecca."

I stood up and wiggled out of my pants, then dropped my panties to the floor. And for the first time in my adult life, I was completely naked in front of someone besides my ex-husband Rob. Well, and the gynecologist.

Lisa's eyes traveled over my body, taking in my lean muscles, the soft swell of my belly, my smallish breasts, my trimmed pussy. She must have liked what she saw because she licked her lips and whispered, "beautiful."

It was everything I didn't know I needed to hear.

"Your turn," I prompted.

She shucked her skirt and underwear, revealing curvy hips, a tiny pooch of a belly, and a small patch of red hair at her apex. Lisa lay down on the bed on her side, then patted the mattress in front of her.

"Get on up here, and position yourself in the opposite direction."

Ah, the sixty-nine position. It had always been one of my favorites, ever since Rob and I saw it in a movie one time. We'd lost our virginity to each other, and over the years we'd had to learn new ways to pleasure each other.

Firmly pushing my ex-husband out of my mind, I lay on the bed, lining up my face with Lisa's pussy, my hips with her face. Even though I was taller, I had long legs, and our torsos lined up almost perfectly.

"You start," Lisa instructed. "Don't think, just feel."

Tentatively I reached out a hand and traced the lips of her pussy. I'd never seen a pussy up close like this, not even mine, and I felt almost fascinated. Slipping one finger inside her slit, I was gratified to find that Lisa was already wet, glad to know that I wasn't alone in this explosive attraction.

I stroked up and down several times, getting a feel for the different terrain of her pussy, then inserted an exploratory finger into her channel. Lisa's hips bucked towards me, and a second later I felt her tongue slid into my pussy.

Pumping in and out of her channel, I leaned forward and licked up her essence. I was surprised by how different she tasted. From time to time I'd tasted myself on my ex-husband's lips or fingers, but Lisa's essence was a little tangier than I remembered tasting from myself.

I found her clit and began circling around it with my tongue, teasing her by getting close but never hitting it full on.

Her hips rocked against my face, and she growled, "Suck my clit."

She didn't have to ask me twice. I captured her clit between my lips, sucking it inside my mouth, and sped up my finger in her channel. Lisa mimicked my actions below, sucking on my clit and fucking me with one finger, then two.

I was already close, but I needed to make her come first. It was my first time doing the full monty with a woman and I was damned well going to make sure she was satisfied. I reached my hand between us and gave the closest breast a firm pinch.

Suddenly she let out a high-pitched wail. Moisture flooded over my finger, Lisa's internal muscles contracting as her orgasm rolled through her. I continued sucking on her clit and fingering her until my own orgasm came.

I was so focused on bringing Lisa pleasure that the orgasm almost snuck up on me. I moaned, fire racing through my veins, my hips rocking against her face until Lisa clamped one hand down on my hip to hold me still.

I was still feeling aftershocks when I slid my finger out of Lisa's pussy. I gave her mound a little squeeze, then flopped over onto my back, breathing heavily.

After a few minutes, Lisa pushed herself to a seated position, looking down at me with a satisfied smile. Her lips were glistening, and when I licked my own lips, I tasted her essence on them.

"You did great, I came really hard," she told me. "Definitely a good effort. How was it for you?"

Life changing, I thought. *The most powerful thing that ever happened to me.*

I hadn't dated in twenty years, but I still knew to never blurt out whatever random thoughts were in your head post-orgasm. Not with someone you didn't know well anyway.

"It was incredible," I finally said.

"Yeah, for a first timer, you really know your way around a vag. How about we do this again sometime?"

Chapter Twelve: The Post-Game Report

When I woke up Sunday morning there was a text from my sister asking if I wanted to join her and Jewel for breakfast. I stretched in my bed, feeling more relaxed than I had been in a long time. I'd almost forgotten how orgasms were such a great stress release.

I threw on some clothes and headed around to the front of the house to access the main entrance. I found them both in the kitchen. Alice was cooking while Jewel squeezed oranges to make fresh juice.

It was the picture of domesticity. I'd wondered how these two would work out when they first got together. Jewel was Alice's best friend's little sister and there was also a bit of an age gap, not to mention the fact that they were very different people. At the time, Jewel had just returned from a stint in the Peace Corps while my sister was a bona fide pencil skirt wearing businesswoman. But damned if they weren't solid as a couple, the perfect match.

And adorable, I thought as Alice walked by and planted a kiss on Jewel's cheek. They shared one of those intimate looks that almost made a person uncomfortable to watch.

"How has your week been?" Jewel asked as we sat down for breakfast. The table was loaded with waffles, berries, bacon, and scrambled eggs.

"Pretty good," I answered, nibbling on a piece of bacon. "Yesterday I met up with this woman that Toya introduced me to."

"Oh yeah, the one who sounded like a dud on the phone," Alice recalled. "Did you like her better in real life?"

"Not really. I mean, she's cute but her personality....ugh. She's a little abrasive and we really have nothing in common."

Except hot sex, I reminded myself.

"That sucks," my sister commiserated. "Well, don't worry, sooner or later you'll find someone you like enough to have sex with."

"Oh, I had sex with her," I smirked.

Alice dropped her fork with a clatter.

"You had sex with someone you don't like?" she clarified, her eyes comically wide.

"Yep." I made an exaggerated P sound.

Alice popped her hands up into the air and cheered like she had just scored the winning touchdown in the Super Bowl.

"You had for-real casual sex! I'm so proud of you!"

I rolled my eyes, and waited for what I knew was coming next...

"How was it?"

"Fan-fucking-tastic." I knew I looked giddy, but I didn't care. "I had no idea pussy tasted so good."

Jewel choked on her juice but didn't comment. Meanwhile my sister looked enthralled.

"How did it all go down?" Alice asked. "Start from the beginning. Don't skip anything."

"We met at the movie theater and we talked a bit, but it was super obvious we didn't really like each other, personality wise, although there were definite sparks. Our knees touched, and then somehow we started making out like teenagers in the back of the movie theater. We made out for a while and then she invited me back to her place."

I paused.

"Despite her abrasive personality, she was very...patient with me when she found out I was inexperienced. And honestly, once we got started, biology just took over and well, let's just say when we finished we were both satisfied."

"That's awesome," my sister said approvingly. "How did you leave it with her?"

"After we finished, we were just kind of recovering on the bed, and then she suggested we get together again. I told her about my 'ten first dates challenge' and I think she thought I was blowing her off or something, because she got really rude."

"Rude how?"

"She got all icy faced and was like, if you don't want to see me again, you don't need to make something up. Honestly, even though the sex was good, I don't like her enough to see her again. I don't want drama in my relationships, so I didn't try to argue with her. I just put on my clothes and left."

We ate in silence for a few minutes before Jewel piped up, "Tell her about what happened with your parents, honey."

"Oh my God! In the excitement over you getting laid I almost forgot!" Alice said. "I had lunch yesterday with Mom and Dad. They're both all wound up about the divorce."

"Shocking," I said wryly.

"Dad is afraid he's supposed to avoid Rob now and he won't have a fishing buddy. He says he hasn't heard from Rob since he got back so his tender feelings are hurt," Alice said sarcastically.

"Rob's waiting for Dad to make the first move, I'm sure."

My ex-husband was one of the most considerate people on Earth. It was one of the things that had made divorcing him so hard. I actually really liked Rob, I just didn't love him. And now that I'd had outstanding sex, I could see that our sex life had been lacking as well.

"That's what I told him," Alice confirmed. "Meanwhile Mom called the girls to comfort them, and she seemed very disappointed to learn that they weren't broken up over your divorce."

My daughters both had level heads, and while they'd been surprised by the divorce when Rob and I told them about it, it didn't really seem to faze them. They both had their own lives, and they knew us well enough to know that the divorce wouldn't impact our relationship with them.

"Poor Mom, it must suck to not have any drama to stir up."

"She'll get over it."

"Your mother just doesn't like things that stray out of her perfect little boxes," Jewel said with an insight that surprised me. "You were the traditional family values daughter, and Alice was the wild lesbian daughter. Alice settling down in a relationship and you going out into the wild messes up both of your pre-defined roles in her mind. It makes her feel off-kilter."

Alice and I both looked at Jewel in amazement.

"Wow, sweetie, that is so insightful," Alice said. "Right on the mark."

"I know," she said smugly. "You remember I'm a trained social worker, right? My entire job is to observe people."

We all jumped as my phone vibrated on the counter, the sound loud in the silence of the kitchen. I got up to check it out in case it was something important.

"Camille and Madison want me to go on a double date with them," I said, looking at the text. "They've got someone they want me to meet."

Chapter Thirteen: The Double Date

Camille and Madison asked me to meet them at a new fusion restaurant in downtown Seattle called "La Caribe". I'd seen a review in the paper. The head chef was some guy who'd won a TV cooking competition, and his new restaurant featured some fancy blend of French and Afro-Caribbean food. It sounded delicious.

In a nod to the restaurant choice, I wore a nicer dress. It was a dark pink with a fitted waist and a skirt that flared out over my calves. I'd paired it with chunky black heels, and pulled my hair up in a twist, leaving a few strands framing my face.

I met the other couple in the lobby, and after trading hugs, I looked around expectantly.

"Seneca is running late," Camille answered my unspoken question. "She got caught up at work. She said we should go ahead and order drinks."

The hostess led us to a table along the windows, two seats on each side. Madison and Camille sat on one side and I sat on the other, leaving a space for my date. I looked around, appreciating the juxtaposition of white table clothes and candles, with Caribbean art on the walls.

"Welcome to La Caribe. Can I get you ladies something to drink?"

I looked up into the bluest eyes I'd ever seen. Our waitress looked to be in her early thirties, with white blonde hair, pale skin, and those incredibly beautiful blue eyes. She definitely had a Nordic heritage, I thought, maybe Norwegian. She was tall and slim but still womanly looking despite her unflattering black pants, white shirt, and server's apron.

For a minute we just stared at each other, everything else seeming to fade away. Then someone cleared their throat, breaking our connection.

"Is it just the three of you?" the waitress asked. She had a name tag that read 'Heidi'. The name suited her.

"No, we're waiting for Rebecca's *date*," Madison told her, sending a clear message.

Our eyes met again for the briefest second before Heidi asked, "What can I get you to drink, Rebecca?"

"I'll have a glass of merlot please," I said.

Heidi got the rest of the drink orders and hustled off, leaving the three of us in silence. It took everything in me not to turn around and watch the waitress. There was just something about her...

"Hi, hi, sorry I'm late."

Seneca came rushing up to the table wearing a power suit and heels, her dark black hair pulled back in a bun so severe I was surprised it hadn't ripped out her hair. She was skinny as a rail with light brown skin, dark eyes, and thin lips that were painted an almost shockingly bright shade of red.

She held out her hand. "You must be Rebecca. I'm Seneca. So nice to finally meet you."

"You too."

There was no spark when I shook her hand, but I reminded myself that sometimes attraction grew over time.

Heidi returned with our drinks, and asked Seneca for her order.

"Here's what I want," Seneca said. "A large tumbler of vodka with about an inch of soda water. Four ice cubes, and two lime slices. Fresh lime only, not lime juice."

Heidi's face didn't change expression but somehow I knew she was trying not to roll her eyes. Her eyes flitted in my direction, and I slightly widened mine like, "Yeah, I know, I heard it." The corner of her mouth quirked.

"Do you know what you want to order for dinner?" Heidi asked. "Or would you like more time?"

After taking Madison and Camille's orders, she turned to me. "I'll take the Rasta Pasta please, with a side of bread."

Seneca's face whipped around in horror.

"Wow, you're brave eating all those carbs." She patted her flat stomach. "If I eat a piece of bread I can't fit into any of my clothes the next day."

I resisted suggesting she buy more forgiving clothes.

Seneca special ordered a salad that was basically nothing but lettuce and tomato with olive oil, then asked for a plain grilled chicken breast with no side dishes. Out of the corner of my eye I saw Camille give Madison a 'what the hell?' look.

The dinner continued along those lines. Seneca seemed to have three obsessions: gaining weight, making money, and her job, in that order. She dominated the conversation, offering her opinion on every topic that came up.

"How do you know Camille and Madison?" I asked, interrupting a long explanation about how Seneca was rebalancing her portfolio to add more mid-cap stocks – whatever the hell that meant.

"My company does business consulting for Madison's leadership team."

I glanced at Madison and Camille, wondering if they were as turned off by Seneca's self-absorbed demeanor as I was. If they were, I couldn't tell.

"Excuse me, I need to go to the restroom," I said, picking up my purse.

It wasn't a lie, I did have to pee, but I figured a break would be good too. I headed to the ladies room to do my business, and when I came out Heidi was in the hallway, leaning against the wall. Her white blonde hair looked luminous in the soft light. She looked around to make sure we were alone.

"I know this is completely inappropriate," she said, one corner of her mouth quirking up. "But when I saw you coming back here, I couldn't help but follow you."

"I'm glad you did."

I moved a little closer, and the air seemed to heat up a bit between us.

"How's your date?" she asked, a little breathlessly.

"She's not my kind of girl. Way too high maintenance."

"Oh, that's too bad," she said, her tone clearly conveying that she was lying.

I smirked.

"Besides, I kind of have a thing for blondes."

I don't know what came over me, but I stepped closer and pressed my lips against hers. I wasn't generally one to initiate contact, but with Heidi, it felt completely right.

She sighed and wrapped her arms around my waist, pulling me closer. I sucked her tongue into my mouth and deepened the kiss. The kiss was somehow both sweet and hot, like a good Thai chili sauce, and I wanted to kiss her forever.

Hearing a door slam somewhere close by, I stepped back, trying hard to get a hold of myself.

"I'm...I'm sorry."

"Don't be sorry," she said with a small smile. "I've been dying to do that since you walked into the restaurant."

"I need to get back to my date," I said regretfully. As much as I wanted to ditch Seneca, I couldn't be rude.

"But would you like to go out sometime? I'd love to see you again. I mean, if you're single."

"I'm single and I'd love that."

I almost sighed in relief.

She took out her order pad and a pen. "Give me your number and I'll call you."

As I headed back to my table, I couldn't help but smile. Maybe this double date wasn't a bust at all.

Chapter Fourteen: Ghosted

"Face it Mom, you've been ghosted."

"Ghosted? What does that mean?"

I looked between my daughters, noting the twin looks of pity on their face. Ironic, given that they were twins. Fraternal twins, but they still looked a lot alike.

"It means that a person has cut off all forms of communication, that they just blow you off," Samantha explained. "Disappears, like a ghost."

She was my oldest, by about four minutes. Like her sister, she was the perfect blend of Rob and me, with my hair and figure, but Rob's eyes and taller height.

"Well, we didn't have any communication to start with," I explained. "We met, she asked for my number and promised to call, and then she didn't. It's been two weeks so I'm assuming she doesn't plan to."

"Ghosted," Skyler repeated.

We were having a mother and daughter spa day at our favorite day spa. We'd already soaked in the hot tubs and gotten massages, and now we were getting mani-pedis. We usually did this once a year as part of the twins' birthday gift.

It was hard to believe that they were turning nineteen tomorrow. I'd gotten pregnant with them right after I began my senior year of high school and they'd been born a few weeks before graduation. Rob and the girls and I had moved in together during my last trimester, renting a garage apartment from my aunt. Despite pressure from our parents, we had waited until the girls were two before we'd gotten married. We didn't want to end up divorced if things didn't work out.

In many ways, we'd all grown up together. Rob and I had been kids ourselves when the girls were born, but we'd been a good parenting team. Looking at my strong, confident college student daughters, I felt happy that we'd done a good job raising them.

Ever since we got here the girls had been quizzing me about my dating progress, delighted to hear about the 'first date challenge' their Aunt Alice had come up with. I'd given them the highlights – and the lowlights – of my dates so far, sparing them from any intimate details of course.

After I told them the story about 'talking' with Heidi in the restaurant hallway, I had to tell them the rest: two weeks had passed without a word from my restaurant crush. I didn't share how many times I'd checked my phone, looking for a phone call or text from Heidi. I didn't want to come off as completely pathetic. It just made no sense to me that the woman had asked for my number so boldly, and then blown me off.

"I really don't understand why she'd ask for my phone number if she wasn't going to call me."

"Are you kidding me, Mom?" Skyler asked. "Guys do that all the time, so why not lesbians?"

"Do what?"

"Ask for your number and then never call you."

"I've asked my guy friends about this," Samantha explained. "They said sometimes they ask because they think the girl is expecting it so they're trying to be nice or just avoid an uncomfortable scene. Plus if they ask you first, you don't have their number to bother them if they're not really interested."

Skyler nodded in agreement.

"Then sometimes it sounds good at the time and then later they decide not to follow up, or they figure, they'll ask for your number in case no one better comes along. Or sometimes they get distracted and don't call, and by the time they think about it, too much time has passed so they ditch the whole thing, so they don't have to explain why it took so long."

I stared at Samantha. "Really? This is how people think?"

"Yeah, and sometimes it's just a game to them, seeing how many numbers they can collect even though they have no intention of calling."

"I don't know, Heidi didn't seem like that kind of person."

I don't know why I was making excuses for her, but sure enough my daughter called me on it.

"Are you saying that you know what kind of person she is just from her serving you pasta and chatting you up in the bathroom hallway?"

I gave Skyler a mock glare. "Fine. Maybe I was wrong."

I didn't feel wrong though. I'd genuinely thought that Heidi and I had a connection. But maybe my daughters and my sister were right: I was too naïve about dating to spot the signs of a player.

"So, you've been on what...five first dates now?" Skyler asked.

"Yeah, and I've got three other women I've been chatting with that I'll be seeing this weekend."

"You're seeing all three of them together?" Samantha asked in confusion.

"No, but it's a holiday weekend so I figured I'd just knock them all out, one each day, and get it over with."

"Well that's the positive attitude you want to go into a date with," Skyler said, shaking her head in exasperation.

"I know. You're right. It's just...I'm starting to question my dating instincts. Your aunt says it's because I have no real dating experience."

"How many guys did you date before Dad?" Samantha asked curiously.

"Like three, and none seriously."

"Yeah," she replied. "You are definitely lacking in dating experience. But you'll get there, Mom. You're relatively attractive and you're not even forty yet. Some woman is bound to snatch you up."

"She doesn't need a woman to be happy," Skyler interjected. "She can be a whole person without being in a relationship. Being single is a perfectly good choice."

I didn't tell her that while I didn't mind being single, I really wanted to have sex again. I only hoped it would happen soon...

Chapter Fifteen: 3 Dates in 3 Days

"You're going on three different first dates in three days?" Alice asked. "That sounds exhausting."

"I had three prospects come in all at once, so I figured, why not?"

"You know, when I gave you this 'Ten First Dates' challenge I didn't expect you'd work through them so quickly. I figured it would take you several months."

"You know me," I joked. "I've always been an overachiever."

The truth was, after only five dates – and one almost date who ghosted me – I was a little bit tired. I had no idea dating would be so challenging. But then again, part of my new life was learning how to date and learning how to date women in particular, so I needed to stick with the program. If I was going to just sit home alone all the time not having sex, I could have stayed married.

For Saturday's date I returned to McTarnahan's, site of my date with Amber, the "weird food" woman, as I liked to think of her.

Bonnie was about five foot six and plump, with permed blonde hair, squinty green eyes, and a nose that was just a little too long and sharp for her face. I knew from our phone conversation that she was in her late forties and worked in the pet store next door to the Morning Jolt coffee shop where Camille worked.

Our conversation flowed pretty easily from the time we sat down. I ordered the hummus platter, thinking of it as a test after the last date I had here, and Bonnie ordered a chicken Caesar salad. And a beer, which seemed like a strange choice for a date that started at eleven-thirty in the morning.

Even stranger, she gulped down half the glass before the waitress left our table, immediately asking for a refill.

I wasn't a teetotaler by any means, but that seemed like a lot of alcohol in such a short time, especially when we were meeting early because Bonnie said she had to go to work this afternoon.

"I thought you said you had to work today?" I couldn't resist asking as she finished off her first beer, wiping the foam off her lip with the back of her hand.

"Yeah, and a couple of drinks really takes the edge off before I go in."

"Is it stressful working at the pet store?" I asked curiously.

"Yeah, all those furry little bastards really get on my nerves. I don't know why people have pets."

Okay, so the pet shop lady hated pets. That was an interesting twist. Needless to say, that date didn't go well, especially when she was half drunk by the time it was over.

On Sunday I met Natalie for a hike. I was looking forward to this date after a great phone conversation. Plus, we'd been connected by my sister-in-law Jewel, who knew me well enough to know what was important to me.

It was a gray and misty day when I arrived at the trailhead. Natalie was there with an adorable pug named Homer. Clearly Natalie didn't hate pets like yesterday's date.

Maybe I should get a pet, I thought to myself. Once Rob finished buying me out of my share of the house, I'd have enough to get myself a nice little townhouse or condo. Maybe a dog or a cat would be nice for companionship.

Well, maybe a cat...

I liked dogs, don't get me wrong, but Homer was one of the most ill-behaved dogs I'd ever met. He barked and lunged at every living thing we passed...squirrels, slugs, other dogs, and humans.

"He won't bite," Natalie told several people while forcibly holding her dog back from going after the person.

I didn't know a lot about dogs, but I was pretty sure when their fur was up and their teeth were showing, they were probably not just saying hello to the passerby.

When Homer wasn't freaking out or trying to kill someone, Natalie and I talked and laughed and generally had a good time. We had a lot of things in common and Natalie was smart and funny.

We hiked for a while until we came to a bench overlooking a canyon, then sat down to rest. Natalie tied Homer's leash to the leg of the bench, and after a few minutes of staring out at the view, Natalie turned to me.

"This is going well," she said sweetly.

She was a petite Chinese woman with silky black hair, smooth skin, and almond-shaped brown eyes. This close, I could see that her nose and upper cheeks were covered in light brown freckles. They were muted, as if she'd tried to cover them up with make-up.

"I'd like to kiss you," she added.

Nodding my permission, I leaned forward and met her halfway. Our lips touched and...suddenly I felt teeth tearing through the pant leg of my yoga pants. A loud, angry growl pierced the air.

I jumped back, bringing Homer with me since he was attached to my pants.

"What the hell?"

"Homer! Down! Bad boy!" Natalie scolded. "You let Rebecca go."

Homer ignored her, forcing Natalie to pry his jaws off my pants. I felt a trickle of blood and realized that he'd scratched my leg with one of his teeth.

"Gosh, I'm sorry Rebecca, Homer gets really jealous when I'm with other people."

She hugged him close and kissed his head like he'd been the one who was almost bitten.

"But you didn't mean it, did you sweetie?" she asked the dog in a high, baby talk voice.

I looked down at the large rip in my expensive Lululemon yoga pants and sighed.

"Should we head back to the car?"

Needless to say, when Natalie suggested that we get together again, I declined.

Call me a glutton for punishment, but on Memorial Day I was back at McTarnahan's for the third date of the holiday weekend.

"So, how do you feel about animals?" I asked Delilah after we ordered our food.

Delilah was a tarot card reader who knew Elizabeth. Apparently they both did readings at the same New Age bookstore. She was a bit older than me, having just turned forty-five, and was actually in a similar place in her life. She had just come out as a lesbian last year and was relatively new to the dating world. I figured if nothing else, we could be friends.

"I like animals," she responded, twisting a long lock of her hair around her finger. Her hair was long and curly, a mixture of black and gray. "Not in a 'I'm a crazy cat lady' way, but more of the normal way."

I nodded. This was promising.

Delilah ordered the hummus platter, so with that barrier out of the way, I was free to order a burger with tater tots. I loved the burgers at McTarnahan's.

"Oh, you eat meat?"

I cringed internally. Was I really on another date with a woman who would police my food choices? We weren't in our early twenties, shouldn't we all be past the food obsessions and crazy diets?

"I eat everything," I said carefully.

Her face pinched but she didn't say anything more, although I caught her looking at my burger in distaste a few times.

We ate our meal in near silence, seemingly running out of things to say, and my efforts to draw Delilah into further conversation mostly didn't work. Maybe the meat thing was a deal breaker for her?

As the waitress cleared our plates I said, "Excuse me, I need to go to the restroom."

"Oh, I get it, you're running out on the bill."

I looked at Delilah in shock. "What are you talking about? I need to pee."

"I've had this happen before," she said bitterly. "Some woman I was on a date with claimed she had to go to the bathroom, then she never came back. Stuck me with the bill."

I looked at her for a long moment, then dug into my wallet and pulled out some cash, more than enough to cover my portion of the bill plus the tip.

"You know, I think we're done here. Have a good day."

I walked back to the car wondering what crazy person I'd meet on my next date...

Chapter Sixteen: This Date Doesn't Count

"Hey Sis, do you want to go to the movies with me and Jewel tonight? They're playing Sixteen Candles, and my dear young wife has never seen our childhood favorite movie."

"Oh, thanks Alice. I'd love to, but I've already got plans tonight."

My sister's face brightened up with interest. She was loving hearing all my crazy dating stories. We'd spent longer laughing about my three dates in three days weekend than I'd spent with the women I went out with.

"Is it a date?"

"Kind of. Rob invited me over for dinner."

"Just so we're clear, going out with your ex-husband does not count as one of your ten first dates."

I rolled my eyes. "Duh. I already had a first date with him, like twenty-one years ago now."

My sister's expression sobered. "Well, I'm glad you two are talking."

"It's not that we weren't talking," I explained. "We've been texting, but I was mostly giving him some space. I know my asking him for a divorce hit him out of the blue, and he needed some time to process everything. But the truth is, I miss my best friend."

A few hours later I was sitting at my old kitchen table in my old kitchen talking to my old friend. After not seeing each other in person for more than two months, I thought things would be awkward, but we immediately fell into the easy conversation that we'd always enjoyed.

"How's work?" Rob asked as he set a tray of lasagna on the table, followed by a giant loaf of garlic bread.

I thought idly that Seneca would break out in hives at the sight of all these carbs. Of course thinking of Seneca made me think of Heidi and how she'd ghosted me, so I pushed them both out of my mind.

"It's good. I've been working a lot of hours because we've been so short-staffed. What about you?"

Rob's family owned a chain of sporting goods stores with locations all across Washington and Oregon.

"Things are finally picking up now that we've moved past all the pandemic closures," he told me. "But our online store is staying steady too, so overall we're doing much better, and our profits are up."

"I'm so glad to hear that."

Rob gave me a questioning look. "I'm going fishing with your dad this weekend."

"Oh good. Dad was really nervous that you guys were breaking up too," I joked. "I think if it came down to it, he wanted custody of you, not me."

Rob smiled. "I'm glad. I really like spending time with him."

My ex-husband's relationship with his own father was more troubled.

We fell silent for a few minutes as we ate our food.

"I'm in therapy," he blurted out suddenly. "It felt weird not talking to you about it, because at first, you were the reason I was there."

"At first?" I asked, taking another bite of my lasagna. My ex was a good cook, much better than me.

"As I've gone through the process with my therapist, I realized that you're not the only one who wasn't totally happy in the marriage. It's not that I was unhappy with you," he rushed to add, "it's more like I was just treading water, you know? Because being with you was comfortable. Familiar."

Impulsively, I reached over and squeezed his hand.

"I know exactly what you mean. It's like we were together for so long, not being together or even having things be different at all, it never entered into our minds. But we never knew if we were missing something better."

"The girls are encouraging me to start dating."

"Really?" I asked in surprise.

I'd assumed that while they felt okay with me dating—since they thought of me as more of a girlfriend than a mother—they'd be a little more protective of their father.

"I'm nervous about it," he confessed. "I haven't been on a date since high school."

"It's really weird out there," I responded without thinking. "Dating is hard."

"You're dating already?" he asked.

His brow crinkled and I knew him well enough to know what he was thinking.

"There was no one I was specifically interested in before we split up," I reassured him. "When I moved into Alice's rental, she was concerned that I would just monkey bar into another relationship. She challenged me to go on at least ten first dates before I accepted a second date with anyone. She's got all her friends fixing me up with women they think I'd like. So...I'm dating."

Rob looked fascinated. "How's it going?"

"Are you sure you're comfortable talking about this?" I asked.

"Sure, you're still my best friend Becky." Rob was the only person in my life who'd ever called me Becky.

"Well, in that case, I have some crazy stories for you. Dating at this age and after so many years being married is a very unusual experience."

Rob and I laughed and finished off a bottle of wine while I told him about each of my dates.

"Dine and Dash Chick is what, number eight?"

I laughed at his description of Delilah. "Yeah, I've got two more to go before I can find a girlfriend or just get some cats and settle into middle age."

Rob met my eyes. My ex was still as handsome as he'd been way back in high school when he first caught my eye, maybe even more.

"You deserve love, Rebecca, and true passion too. We both do. I have a feeling we'll both find it soon."

"I hope you're right, Rob."

Suddenly he snapped his fingers. "There's this new clerk at the store who just broke up with her girlfriend, she's super cute..."

I held up my hand. "I think that would cross the line there, buddy. Let's both try to find our new loves the old-fashioned way...through friends and dating apps."

Chapter Seventeen: Just Passing Through

"Where are you going all fancy?"

My sister and Jewel were decked out in running clothes. They stopped as they approached my car. Jewel looked fresh as a daisy, but my sister looked like she was fixing to pass out. Her face was red, and her damp hair was plastered to her forehead. I suppressed a smile. It wasn't easy keeping up with a younger wife.

"I have a government accountants conference," I told them, modeling what I thought of as my "conference dress."

It was a sedate black dress with a white collar and white blouse, that I'd paired with low black kitten heels. It was much nicer than anything I'd wear to my mostly casual workplace.

Alice made a show of giving me a large, fake yawn. "A government accountants conference? Good Lord, that's the most boring thing I've ever heard."

I smirked. My sister had never understood my love of numbers.

"Well, I'm excited about it. An old friend that I used to work with is the keynote speaker. She's going to talk about public transparency in government accounting."

Alice mimed throwing up, and Jewel poked her in the side with her elbow.

"I hope you have a good conference," Jewel said politely.

"I don't understand how you are the most mature one in this relationship," I told my sister-in-law. Jewel was seven years younger than Alice.

"It's not hard, believe me."

"That's what she said," Alice snickered. On some levels, my sister was a thirteen year old boy. Her favorite thing was a fart joke.

"Okay then, on that note, I'm out of here."

I got into my car with a wave, then drove to the convention hotel in downtown Seattle. After finding a parking spot in the cavernous garage, I headed to registration. It didn't take long to sign in and get my conference materials. I looked around the ballroom area, which was packed with conference goers, wondering if I'd run into anyone I knew here.

"Rebecca!"

I turned to greet my old friend with a smile. Janelle and I had worked together until about ten years ago when she was recruited to work as an accountant at one of the big firms back east. She'd moved to Washington D.C. for her new job, but we'd stayed connected a bit via social media. I'd reached out to her as soon as I'd seen her name on the conference speaker's page, hoping to reconnect.

After giving me a big hug, Janelle asked if I could meet her for dinner.

"I'm booked up most of the day, but I would love to catch up tonight if you're free."

"That sounds great."

By the time the day ended, I was exhausted from talking to people and attending seminars. Still, I was looking forward to reconnecting with my old friend. We met in the hotel lobby and headed over to a restaurant two blocks away that had a great menu.

After ordering our drinks, Janelle gave me a long look, her expression sympathetic.

"I heard through the grapevine that you got divorced. I'm so sorry. I know you and Rob were together for a long time."

"Oh thanks, I appreciate that. But it's all good, our divorce was very amicable."

"Is it too nosy for me to ask what happened?" she asked.

"Not at all," I replied. "It's not that exciting, really. One day I realized that I'd been lying to myself and my husband. I'm a lesbian."

For some reason, Janelle didn't look as surprised as most of the other people I'd told about my revelation.

"You know, I always wondered if you were a lesbian, or at least bi," she told me.

I was shocked. "What? Why?"

"I can't really explain it. I just have a good intuition, like some kind of a gaydar or whatever, for these things. For some reason, I always got lesbian vibes from you, but since you were married, I figured either I was wrong, or you weren't out yet."

We paused while the waitress came back with our drinks and took our food orders, both of us going with the salmon special.

"I think you'll love the food here," I told Janelle. "I've been here a few times, and everything's always been delicious."

"Seattle's food scene is so much better than D.C.'s," she said wistfully. "I miss restaurants that are focused on food instead of networking. Anyway, back to your divorce. Did you meet someone? Is that why you realized the truth?"

I shook my head. "Not really, it just kind of hit me at the gym one day when I realized I was checking out all the women there and hadn't given any of the guys a second look."

Janelle laughed.

"So, I broke the news to my husband and moved into my sister's basement rental. This was a few months ago. Since then, I've been dating and trying to figure out who I am if I'm not someone's wife. It's been interesting, especially at this age, but it's also been fun."

"Well good for you."

Our dinner came and we spent the rest of the meal sharing dating stories.

"I think you win," I told Janelle as she finished a particularly crazy story. "Although you've had years more of dating time to get through. Do you think you'll find someone you want to settle down with sometime?"

"Maybe."

"What about you? Are you eager to settle down again? Or do you think you'll play the field for a while?"

"I'm in no hurry. In fact, my sister challenged me to go on at least ten first dates before I accepted a second date, just to make sure I wasn't jumping into something too quickly."

"Really?" Janelle leaned forward and put her hand on mine. "I have a confession to make then. I used to have a big crush on you, back when we worked together."

My eyes flew to hers. "You did? I had no idea. I didn't even know you were gay."

"Yeah, I never mentioned it because you seemed like you were happily married. Plus, I didn't want to make you uncomfortable if I was wrong about your sexual orientation."

"Mostly I was happily married," I confirmed. "I just didn't realize that I wanted more."

She squeezed the hand that covered mine. It felt warm and strong.

"What would you think about coming up to my hotel room to continue this conversation?"

Chapter Eighteen: Kissing My Friend

"Let's go."

Deciding to take Janelle up on her invitation to go up to her hotel room, we paid our bill and headed out. We made our way back from the restaurant in silence, walking close enough that our shoulders were touching with every step.

Hearing she had a crush on me was a total surprise. Either she was a good actress, or I'd been clueless – or both. I mean, of course I'd noticed her, even back then. She had a tight body, despite the fact that she'd just turned forty, with an adorable dark brown pixie cut, brown eyes, and an olive complexion that hinted at a Mediterranean heritage.

We didn't say a word the entire way back to the hotel, but when we got into the elevator up to her room she reached one small hand out and wrapped her fingers in mine. I gave her hand a gentle squeeze.

Janelle's hotel room was one of those generic rooms, nice, but nothing special. I glanced around, taking in the neatly made king-sized bed, a small loveseat a few feet away, and a large flat-screen TV on the opposite wall.

"Shall we sit down?" Janelle asked, patting the cushion next to her as she gracefully dropped into the loveseat.

I still wasn't one hundred percent sure if we were coming up here to talk or fuck. I also wasn't sure which option I preferred. I liked Janelle, and I thought she was attractive, but I wasn't sure that I was attracted to her specifically. Then again, I'd just found out that she was a lesbian, so I was still a bit shocked.

"Thanks for dinner," I said.

"No problem, thanks for the recommendation. My salmon was incredible."

As Janelle spoke, one hand slid along the back of the loveseat behind me, her fingers trailing down to caress my shoulder. I turned to face my friend. She had a soft, rueful look on her face.

"After having a crush on you for so long, I feel a little weird about making a move," she confessed.

I shifted sideways, bringing one hand up to cup the back of her head, then brought my lips to hers. Janelle sat completely still. I licked along the seam of her lips, then dipped my tongue inside her mouth, sliding it against hers. I threaded my fingers through her short hair with one hand, bracing myself on the couch with the other.

The movement of my tongue on hers seemed to jolt Janelle out of her trance, because she shifted to face me more fully, one hand coming to my hip, and then she was kissing me back.

It still fascinated me how kissing a man and a woman seemed exactly the same but felt so very different. Janelle's lips were soft, the skin around her face smooth.

It was...okay.

We made out for a few minutes, but I wasn't really getting excited. When I'd kissed Veronica and Lisa, my body had immediately tingled with excitement. My panties had soaked with arousal.

But with Janelle I felt...nothing. I mean, it was nice enough, but I wasn't having the physical reaction I would have hoped for. We pulled apart, eyes meeting.

"That was a little anticlimactic," Janelle said.

Her eyes widened as if she hadn't meant to say that out loud. "I'm so sorry! I just meant..."

"You're not actually attracted to me the way you thought you were?" I guessed.

"It's not that, exactly, it's more that there's no...spark I guess. It didn't get my heart racing. Did you feel anything?"

"Not a thing," I confirmed, my tone almost cheerful. "Let's try one more time, just in case."

I leaned forward to kiss her again, and her hand came to my left boob, cupping me gently through the fabric of my dress while she kissed me back. This time we only kissed for a moment, before pulling away again.

"Nothing," Janelle confirmed.

"I guess we're destined to be just friends," I said.

"Yeah. Oh well, at least we tried. How would you feel about ordering dessert from room service?"

I laughed at her rapid change in topic.

"Sounds like a plan."

I hung out with Janelle for a while, both of us back to the easy connection we'd shared before she'd confessed about her crush. When I left we exchanged hugs and a promise to keep in better touch.

As I drove home, I realized that I was glad tonight had happened. It wasn't like I'd had a crush on Janelle or anything, so there'd been no sense of loss in finding out that we weren't physically attracted to each other. She'd seemed fine with how things turned out too, joking around later that she would have hated to have a long-distance relationship anyway.

Tonight had taught me about really tuning into my body and emotions, and feeling safe being honest about what I was feeling. Looking inward, I realized that I wasn't desperate to date someone, and I wasn't desperate for a new relationship. It would happen when it happened.

I had one more date left to prove my sister wrong. I knew that part of her stupid challenge idea was the belief that I wasn't emotionally mature enough to differentiate between passion and love. That I couldn't be alone, after never being alone in my life.

I appreciated her concern, but she was wrong. Not only could I be alone, but I was actually looking forward to it. I relished the idea in fact.

One of Alice's friends had just texted me the phone number of a new woman she wanted to fix me up with. Assuming she didn't sound like a total psycho on the phone, I'd suggest we get together for coffee.

And once I'd gotten the coffee date out of the way, I was going to spend the next several months focused just on myself. I wasn't going to actively look for people to date, wasn't going to ask people to fix me up with their friends. If I found someone, it would be the old-fashioned way: by luck.

Little did I know that luck was about to laugh in my face.

Chapter Nineteen: Was It Something I Said?

Date number ten proved to be a bit elusive.

I called one woman, and it was clear that we were not going to get along. With Lisa there had at least been a spark of passion beneath the dislike – I still fantasized about that night we had sex when I was alone with my vibrator. But my call with Joanie was such a dud we didn't even bother trying to get together.

Jewel met another woman at work who she thought I'd mesh with, but then she discovered that the woman had gotten back with her ex-girlfriend.

A couple of weeks went by before someone else gave me a prospect, which was fine. A friend of a friend of Alice's connected me with a woman named Mary. We played phone tag and texted a few times before I finally just suggested we set a time to meet for coffee at Morning Jolt.

It seemed appropriate that the first and last dates of the challenge would both happen at Camille's coffee shop. Plus, since we hadn't actually been able to talk on the phone, I didn't want to commit to anything more than coffee with Mary in case things didn't go well.

When I got to the coffee shop, I didn't see anyone sitting alone, so I got myself a chai latte and settled in at a table. Five minutes later a woman strode in, looked around, and headed straight for my table.

She was tall and plus sized, with super short hair, like crew cut short, a hoop nose ring, and one of those large disks stretching the flesh of her left earlobe. She was wearing a tight white tank top that revealed two full sleeves of tattoos, cargo pants, combat boots, and a plaid flannel that she'd tied around her waist. No doubt that part was some kind of fashion statement since it was the middle of summer and already pushing ninety degrees outside.

No one would mistake this woman as straight, I thought drily.

"Rebecca?" she asked.

"Yes, hi Mary, it's nice to meet you."

I stood up to shake her hand, sending her a friendly smile and trying not to wince at her firm grip. Her hand was warm and a little clammy.

Mary looked me up and down, taking in my floral summer skirt, flat sandals, and plain but flattering white scoop-necked tee shirt. Her lip curled slightly, telling me that she didn't like what she saw. I realized that there was another small hoop in her upper lip.

I have to admit that the look smarted a bit, given that I'd taken some care with my appearance. Camille had complimented my outfit when she'd taken my order at the counter earlier.

"What are you drinking there?" Mary asked gruffly, nodding towards my coffee.

"A coconut milk chai latte?" For some reason it came out as a question. This woman's odd behavior was throwing me off.

A look of derision crossed Mary's round face.

"Yeah, sorry, this isn't going to work."

"What?" I asked in confusion.

Mary scowled, pointing at herself, then jabbing a blunt finger in my direction.

"You. Me. There's no way this works so there's no reason for either of us to waste our time here. Good luck though."

I stood there with my mouth open as she marched away without another word. What the hell had just happened? I mean, our physical appearances were very different, but that didn't mean we couldn't have been compatible. Maybe?

Did this count as date ten if the woman ditched me as soon as she saw me?

As Mary left, another woman came in the door, her blue eyes immediately shooting in my direction. I realized with a start it was

Heidi, the waitress who had asked for my number and then ghosted me a few months ago.

Is today "Humiliate Rebecca Day"? I wondered.

Today Heidi was dressed casually in loose shorts and a tee shirt, her blonde hair pulled up in a high ponytail that made her look young and summery. Her skin was a little darker now, like she'd been outside tanning during our unusually warm summer, but still pale.

Heidi's strikingly blue eyes were wide with shock as she came over to me. I knew the feeling. What were the chances that I'd run into the same woman twice, several months apart, while on a terrible date? Seattle wasn't the biggest city, but it wasn't small either. You didn't run into the same people frequently.

"Rebecca?" she called as she hurried in my direction. "Oh my God, I'm so glad we ran into each other again!"

Heidi looked genuinely happy to see me, which made me feel kind of warm and fuzzy until I remembered how she had seemed so interested in me when I'd kissed her in the restaurant hallway. Interested enough to ask for my phone number, but not interested enough to ever call me, I reminded myself.

I plopped down in my chair and took a bracing sip of my chai latte. It was delicious. I couldn't believe I'd just been disparaged for liking tea. Would things have turned out differently today if I'd dressed more androgynously or ordered a black coffee? Not that I cared really – Mary's rudeness would have been a deal breaker for me anyway – but I was a little curious.

Heidi came to stop by my table. I didn't even bother looking at her.

"If you don't mind, I've already been ditched once today. I'd really rather be alone."

Heidi ignored my sad words, sitting in the chair across from me. I looked up and met those brilliant blue eyes.

"Just hear me out, Rebecca. Please."

Chapter Twenty: Second Chances

Heidi looked so earnest, I couldn't help but hear what she had to say. Just seeing her again made my lips tingle with the memory of that brief kiss we'd shared in the restaurant hallway all those months ago.

"Have you ever been a waitress?" she asked.

That wasn't what I expected her to lead with.

"Years ago," I acknowledged. "I waitressed in college. Why?"

"When you came into the restaurant that night, I was immediately attracted to you," she started. "You were on your date with that horrible woman. After hearing the two of you introduce yourselves I figured out that it was just some kind of a set-up with your friends, so I bided my time hoping I could get you alone."

"You did get me alone," I reminded her.

Her fair complexion turned a little pink, like she was remembering our kiss the same as I was. A kiss that I'd been the one to initiate.

"Yeah, well, I don't know if you remember this, but when I asked for your number, I wrote it on my order pad."

I looked upward, trying to remember if that was true, then nodding when I realized that it was.

"When you're a waitress, there are always a bunch of order pads laying around, you just grab whatever one is laying around. Everyone basically shares them. Was it like that when you were a waitress?"

"Yeah, I think so."

"Well, after I got your number, the restaurant got really slammed. We had a table of twenty come in without a reservation, then we just had table after table come in. There was a line up the block."

"I remember."

Everyone at my table had been glad we'd gotten our food before the large group came in, taking over most of the small space in the dining room. The noise level had risen dramatically, making it hard to even talk.

"At some point I must have set down the order pad that I wrote your number in, and someone else picked it up. I was so busy I didn't think anything about it but then when I was getting off shift, I remembered that I'd written your number in one of the books."

"You're saying you lost my number?" I clarified.

Her explanation was plausible, but should I believe her?

"I went from waitress to waitress, demanding to see their books, looking for your number, but I never found it. I don't know if someone threw it out or wrote over it or what, with all the chaos that night, no one remembered anything."

"You lost my number," I repeated. "That's why you didn't call?"

"Yes. It was stupid, and I've cursed myself a hundred times since then for not ripping the paper out of the pad and putting it in my pocket where it would have been safe."

Her face looked open. Earnest.

"I was thinking about you that entire night, wondering if you were going to go home with that other woman, feeling super jealous even though I didn't have a right to."

My core tingled at her words.

"No way, she was way too high maintenance for me. She seemed like the kind of woman who wouldn't go down on you because she'd be afraid she'd ingest some carbs when you came."

We both burst out laughing.

"I'm sure you thought I was some asshole who asked for people's numbers and then just didn't call."

"I did, yeah," I admitted.

"Can I make it up to you?" she asked.

I drained the rest of my chai. "What did you have in mind?"

"Do you have some time to hang out now?"

"Well, I just got ditched by a blind date who apparently hated me on first sight, so yeah, I've got time."

Her lips twitched.

"What a stupid, stupid woman. But her loss is my gain. May I buy you a refill?"

"Sure. I'll have a coconut milk chai latte please."

She gave me a wide smile. "Hey! That's my drink too."

I watched her as she went up to the counter, chatting with Camille. I wondered idly why Camille was working as a barista when her billionaire girlfriend owned this place and a successful tech company, but I guess it wasn't really my business.

"Here you go."

Heidi's return pulled me out of my thoughts. She slid my cup over, then took a sip of her own chai. A bead of foam dotted her upper lip, and it took everything in me not to lean across the table and lick it off.

"At the risk of being trite, tell me about yourself Rebecca."

We chatted for the next hour, the conversation flowing easily. I felt totally comfortable with her in a way that I hadn't felt on any other date. I told her about my job and my divorce and my sister's Ten First Dates challenge. In return I learned that in addition to being a waitress, Heidi was in graduate school, getting her degree in social work.

"My sister-in-law is a social worker," I shared.

"I can't wait to meet her," Heidi replied.

I liked how she assumed that she and Jewel would meet someday. My sister Alice's voice echoed in my head, warning me that my inexperience with dating in general and women in particular would make me vulnerable to falling in love too easily.

I wouldn't say that was how I felt about Heidi, but I could definitely sense a future with her. A rightness. She was one of only a couple of women I'd dated since the divorce who I even wanted to see again, and the first one to make me think about the future.

An alarm sounded from Heidi's phone.

"I set my phone to remind me when it was time to go home and get ready for work," she explained. "I was afraid I'd get distracted by you."

Her eyes met mine. "I definitely am distracted by you."

We exchanged goofy smiles, then Heidi held up her phone.

"Can I get your number again? I swear I'll call you this time. I'm putting your number right in my phone this time, so nothing happens to it."

I rattled off my digits and a few seconds later I heard my own phone ding in my purse.

"I texted you, so you have my number as well," she explained.

"Great."

I was dying to ask her out, wanting to see her again, but it felt important that she make the next move after what happened. I wasn't disappointed.

"Any chance you're free tomorrow night?" she asked.

"I am."

She looked thrilled.

"Can we have dinner or something?"

"Sounds good."

Heidi stood up and so did I. She pulled me into a long hug, her head pressed against mine. She smelled like sunshine. As she pulled away, she gave me a soft smile.

"I'll text you when I'm on break to hash out the details."

"Okay."

"Oh, and Rebecca?"

"Yeah."

"I hope you're done with your Ten First Dates thing, because I'm telling you right now, I want to be your last first date."

Chapter Twenty-One: We Had "The Night"

The minute I walked into my sister's place she pounced.

"Who was the blonde leaving your apartment this morning, you dirty little slut?"

"Really? Is that language necessary?" I asked, pushing past her to enter the house.

"Hey Jewel," I greeted my sister-in-law.

She sent me a teasing look. "Alice has been dying to bug you about the blonde. I held her back as long as I could."

My sister shoved a glass of red wine into my hand and pointed to a stool by the kitchen island.

"Come on now, spill. I'm just a boring old married woman now, I need to live vicariously through you."

"Hey!" Jewel cried out in mock outrage. "I ought to paddle your ass for that."

I tried not to wince at the visual that created in my mind. This wasn't the first time I'd gotten a glimpse into that particular dynamic in my sister's relationship with her younger wife.

Alice patted her shoulder. "Just kidding, honey. You're all the excitement I need."

She leaned towards Jewel and whispered into Jewel's ear, still loud enough for me to hear. "But feel free to punish me later anyway."

I groaned, and Alice's attention turned back to me.

"I still want to hear about Rebecca's night of debauchery."

"There was no debauchery," I told her. "We just talked...and snuggled a little."

My sister looked skeptical, but as usual, Jewel was the voice of reason. "We'd love to hear more, if you're willing to share."

I told them the story over dinner. Date number nine at the coffee shop Saturday. That woman Mary taking one look at me and ditching me. Heidi walking in as Mary left Morning Jolt. Her explanation about losing my number with her order pad.

"She messaged me on her break that same day, then we texted back and forth most of Saturday night when she got off work. Things were going well, so I offered to cook her dinner after she got off work on Sunday."

Alice coughed into her hand. *"Slut."* I ignored her jab.

"I figured after spending an entire day waiting tables, she wouldn't want to head into another restaurant for our date," I explained.

"What did you make her?" Jewel asked.

Alice shot her an exasperated look but didn't comment.

"I made a taco bar and then we ate tacos and drank beer while we watched a few episodes of 'Sex and the City' on the couch."

"The original series, I hope."

"Of course," I answered my sister's question.

"So, you were watching 'Sex and the City'...," she prompted. "And then...?"

"In between episodes we just...talked."

I couldn't help the smile that lit up my face.

"It was so great. We talked about anything and everything. We talked until like three o'clock in the morning, and then we fell asleep snuggled together on the couch."

I held up my hand as my sister opened her mouth. "Fully clothed."

"Oh my God, you had 'the night'!" My sister looked thrilled.

"The night?" I asked. "What do you mean?"

"Remember that episode of Friends where Joey is up all night talking to a woman and then Monica explains the significance of having a night that's all talking?"

"Vaguely."

"You know what I'm talking about. The night where you can't stop talking to each other, where you connect on such a cellular level it almost feels like you'll never get enough of the person."

Alice was right, it had felt just like that.

"So, what happened after you fell asleep?"

"We slept," I said, deliberately misunderstanding Alice's question.

She gave me an impatient look.

"We slept through the night and didn't get up until my alarm went off this morning. I told her that I had to get ready for work, kissed her goodbye, and she left."

I didn't tell Alice that waking up with Heidi cuddled into my back had been heavenly. That seeing her sleepy eyes looking up at me had made me feel a rush of emotion I could scarcely interpret.

And I certainly didn't tell her that the only thing that had kept our wandering hands and lips from moving things to the next level this morning was the blare of my back-up alarm reminding me that I had to get myself dressed and ready for work so I wouldn't be late for our staff meeting.

"Are you sure you didn't have sex?" my sister asked suspiciously.

The woman was like a horny dog with a bone.

"I think I would have remembered if I did."

"Not at all? There were no orgasms?"

"No, we made out and got a little handsy, but neither of us seemed to be in a hurry to move things to the next level."

I held up my hand, anticipating my sister's next question.

"We are both very attracted to each other, that's super obvious. It was like we had this unspoken agreement to develop intimacy before we actually got intimate, you know?"

Again my mind flashed to kissing Heidi on the couch this morning, her firm hand kneading my breast over the fabric of my shirt. The feel of the damp crotch of her panties sliding against my thigh while we'd moved together.

"That's good," my sister said. "Really good. There's no reason to sleep together on the first date. You should never do that."

"We slept together on the first date," Jewel reminded her.

My sister's face flushed. "That was different."

"How?" Jewel and I asked in unison.

"It just was, okay? I already knew you, for one thing. And you'd gotten me all discombobulated when you did that thing with your foot in the restaurant..."

I grabbed my sister's arm and squeezed. "Please. I'm begging you not to finish that sentence."

"When are you going to see her again?" Jewel asked, saving the day as usual, although the look she sent my sister was downright filthy.

"I was in a hurry to get ready for work, and she's working right now. We agreed to check in tonight and see when our schedules align for another date."

Alice raised one eyebrow in question.

"She's working full-time and going to school full-time, so her schedule is a little tight."

"What a minute, exactly how young is she?" Alice asked, a trace of judgement in her voice that was unfounded given that her wife was considerably younger than her.

"She's thirty-four, not that it's your business," I said firmly. "She decided to go back to school after her divorce."

"I'm glad you had a good night with her," Jewel piped up. "Maybe she'll be the one."

"I think she might be."

I was lying. There was no 'might' about it. Heidi was the woman I wanted to spend the rest of my life with.

Chapter Twenty-Two: The Third Date

"When are you seeing Ghost Girl again, Mom?"

I rolled my eyes, even though Skyler couldn't see me through the phone.

"Her name is Heidi, and we're going out again on Sunday night."

I hadn't seen her since she'd left my apartment early Monday morning, but we'd talked and texted multiple times a day ever since then. Finding a time to get together was difficult, between her schedule and mine, but we'd made plans to have an early dinner after Heidi got off work at the restaurant Sunday afternoon.

"This is your third date, right?"

I thought for a minute. "Yeah, I guess so. If we count the coffee shop meeting as our first date..."

"We do," Skyler said confidently.

"Then last Sunday would be our second date, and this week would be our third. Why?"

Instead of answering me, I heard her call out to her sister, "Mom's going on her third date with someone Sunday. It's the woman who ghosted her that one time. But it turns out it was all a mistake."

"Tell her to wax," I heard Samantha reply.

"I don't wax," I told Skyler before she could pass on her sister's advice. "I like things down there to be the way God intended."

My daughter gave me the aggrieved sigh I hadn't heard since she was a teenager. "Gross."

"Why are you asking about which date it is?" I asked, trying to redirect her from the state of my lady box, which was well groomed despite the lack of waxing, thank you very much.

"The third date is the sex date Mom. Everyone knows that."

"I thought that was just a 'Sex and the City' thing."

"No, it's a dating thing," Skyler told me with exaggerated patience. "So if you're not going to wax, you'd better at least clean things up down there. And shave your legs."

I couldn't believe I was taking dating advice from my daughters.

"Is this our third date?" I asked Heidi over dinner that night.

We'd met at McTarnahan's, the site of two of my worst dates. I figured that, like the coffee shop, if I had a good date with Heidi here it would take away the bad juju at the restaurant. Then I could enjoy my hummus platters and tater tots there again in the future.

Or maybe it was a test. Things had been going so well between us, it almost seemed too easy.

When we were seated I'd been tempted to order the hummus platter as another test, but I already knew that Heidi wasn't a fussy eater, so I went with what I was hungry for instead. For her part, Heidi showed absolutely no interest in what I was ordering.

"Yes, I'm thinking this would be our third official date," Heidi answered my question. "I mean, I guess we could count the first time we met since there was a kiss involved, but that wasn't really a date. Not with each other, anyway."

She cocked her head, her white blonde hair sliding towards her shoulder. She was wearing a cute summer dress tonight and had left her hair down in loose waves. She looked so freaking beautiful it took my breath away.

"Why do you ask?"

I grimaced. "It's just something my daughter said."

"She wanted to know if we were going to sleep together tonight?" she guessed.

"Yeah."

Heidi leaned forward and met my eyes. My eyes dropped to the cleavage this movement revealed before dutifully going back to look at her face.

"Well, I've been wearing out my vibrator ever since I met you, so I definitely wouldn't say no to sex tonight," she answered earnestly. "But we don't have to do anything you're not ready for. We can wait if you want to. I've never felt this way about anybody, Rebecca. I'm sorry if that sounds too clingy or whatever, but it's the truth."

I breathed out a sigh of relief. The fact was that I'd been thinking about Heidi all week. Dreaming of her all week. Chastising myself for getting too serious about her all week. It felt good to know that I wasn't alone in this.

"Do you want to come home with me tonight?" I asked softly. "We can just...see where things go."

"More than anything."

We took our time finishing up our food, neither of us in a rush now that we knew the outcome of the evening was inevitable. After we paid the check, we walked out of the restaurant hand-in-hand, fingers intertwined.

When we exited the building, I couldn't help but swing her around and press her up against the brick wall a few feet away from the entrance.

"What are you doing?" she asked breathlessly. Her eyes were trained on my lips, telling me it was a rhetorical question. I pressed my pelvis against hers, noting how our bodies lined up almost exactly.

"What I've wanted to do all night."

Giving her time to stop me – while hoping desperately that she wouldn't stop me – I slowly leaned forward and pressed my lips against hers. Heidi sighed and opened for me immediately, and I swept my tongue into her mouth, tasting the sweetness of the marionberry pie that we'd shared for dessert.

When she kissed me back, I gripped her shoulders, moving closer. Her hands went to my waist, then slid down lower, coming around to cup my ass cheeks, kneading them between her fingers as the kiss went on and on. When we finally broke apart, we were both breathing heavily, and my nipples were so engorged that they felt painful.

"Oh my God," she whispered. "How can this feel so good?"

I chuckled against her neck, where I was kissing a path down to her shoulder.

"I know, right?"

Heidi grabbed my face between her hands, lifting my head so we were face-to-face again.

"Rebecca, if you don't take me home with you right now, I'm going to have no choice but to strip you naked, lay you on the ground, and grind against you until we both come our brains out."

My pussy spasmed, a rush of arousal flooding the crotch of my panties.

"Can't have that happening," I said, pointing to the sign above her head. "I know this used to be Mrs. Basil's School for Wayward Girls, but they've really cleaned the place up since then."

"Meet you at your place?" she asked. "It's closer than mine."

"I'll race you."

Chapter Twenty-Three: Feels Like Making Love

When Heidi pulled up on the street behind me, I jumped out of my car, pulling her door open before she even turned off the car.

"Someone is a little eager," she teased as I threaded my fingers through hers and dragged her towards the entrance to my apartment on the side of the house.

Unable to wait a second longer, I pressed her against the house, laying a fast kiss on her lips. She giggled.

"We need to stop meeting like this. Let's take this show inside."

We rushed into the house, tearing at each other's clothes before the door was even closed. Kissing and groping, we headed into the bedroom. Coming to a stop near the bed, I looked at Heidi's luscious breasts, encased by white lace.

I cupped them in my hands, boosting them up a bit before easing them back down and sliding my hands behind her to unclasp the bra. She tugged it down her shoulders, freeing her milky white breasts. I couldn't resist lowering my head to swipe my tongue across the hard peaks of her dark pink nipples.

"I can't decide what I want to do to you first," I confessed, looking up at her from beneath my eyelashes.

"Well, I have no such hesitancy," she teased. "I want you to ride my face."

She stepped back, still fully dressed from the waist down, and lowered herself to the bed, propping her head up with one of my pillows.

When I just stood there gaping at her she called, "Lose the clothes and get on up here, Rebecca."

Dropping the shirt that was half on and half off, I shucked my linen pants, underwear, and bra, standing naked in front of her for the first time. Her eyes darkened as she licked her lips. I'd never felt so beautiful.

I moved onto the bed, crawling over her on hands and knees, and leaned down to suck one of her nipples into my mouth. I circled it with my tongue, then closed my lips around the tip until she started squirming beneath me. After doing the same to the other side, I crawled past her shoulders, gripped the bed frame, and slowly lowered my pussy over her face.

Heidi's hands immediately came to my hips, pulling me down so she could explore my folds with her tongue. She licked me over and over again, moving from top to bottom, before circling my opening.

I sighed as she slid her tongue inside me, then pulled me even closer to her head so she could go deeper. I gripped the headboard and ground my pussy against her face, reveling in the feeling of her tongue fucking me from below.

When I was a quivering mess of need, Heidi reached her hands up and grabbed my breasts, one in each hand. She squeezed hard, kneading my flesh roughly, while continuing to spear me with her tongue.

I had to admire her ability to multitask, because right now it was taking all of my concentration to remain upright.

My clit throbbed in time with my heartbeat, craving some of the action, and as if she'd heard its silent call, Heidi slid her hands back downward, one hand moving to grip my hip while the other found my clit, circling and pressing on it with her fingers.

It was the bit of extra pressure I needed to let go, and I came with a long groan of her name. When she'd first suggested I sit on her face I'd worried that I might smother her or something, but now I was so far gone I didn't care. I was completely mindless, focused only on taking the pleasure she was offering with her tongue and her fingers.

I felt my orgasm come like a lightning strike, electrifying my entire body, making me shake with the force of it.

"Heidi," I gasped as I shuddered against her face, trying to draw out my pleasure as long as I could.

As the waves of my release subsided, I slid off her and moved down until I could lay my head on her shoulder. I felt completely spent, unable to move a muscle. But then I glanced up at her face, and I could see my essence glistening on Heidi's face.

It was all I needed to recover.

I moved over her, slowly making my way down her body, leaving a trail of kisses on her sternum, and over her belly. Keeping my lips on her skin, I pulled off her pants and underwear, tossing them over my shoulder as I continued moving downward.

Bypassing her pussy, I kissed my way down the inside of one leg, and up the other. The minute I was close enough to her apex again, Heidi grabbed my hair – hard – and tried to direct me to where she wanted me.

"Impatient?" I teased as I stared at her pussy. It was lovely and pink, almost the same color as Veronica's vagina sculpture, with a tuft of light blonde hair right at the top.

She levered up to her elbows and gave me a mock glare.

"I've wanted you since the moment I saw you, Rebecca," she said impatiently. "It feels like I've been waiting for you forever."

I gave her a smile, then spread her legs wide. Kneeling between them, I sat on my heels and pulled her hips up onto my thighs. Heidi dropped her upper body back onto the bed with a sigh.

Holding her hip with one hand, I explored the folds of her pussy with the other. Starting with the outer lips, I ran the pads of my fingers up and down, then slid in between, finding her dripping with arousal.

I scooped up some moisture, then brought a finger to my lips, sucking it into my mouth as I stared into her blue eyes.

"Delicious," I said.

Heidi made a strangled sound.

I traced up and down her channel again and again, gradually picking up the pace until Heidi was bucking against my hands. Then, and only then, did I slide my index finger into her channel, pumping in and out slowly.

She sighed, and I added a second finger and increased the speed. Heidi punched her hips up with every stroke, meeting my questing fingers. Her inner muscles squeezed tight around them, as if she was afraid I'd remove my fingers before finishing the job.

Pressing my other hand into the soft tissue of her mound, I moved my thumb to swipe it back and forth against her clitoris, adding a pressure that made her whine.

"I got you, baby."

I rotated the fingers that were inside her, until I found the rough patch that made her damn near levitate off the bed. I stroked her G spot while pressing down hard on her clit with my thumb. Within thirty seconds, Heidi found her release, bucking so hard I thought she was going to throw me right off the bed.

Her head whipped back and forth, and she shook violently until she reached the end of her release and collapsed down as if she was boneless. I eased my hands away from her body, then moved up the bed to snuggle her into my side.

Heidi placed her head on my chest and wrapped one arm around my waist, her bare legs tangling with mine.

The last thing I heard before we fell asleep was Heidi whispering something that sounded a lot like "I love you."

Chapter Twenty-Four: Making It Official

"So is Heidi your girlfriend now?"

I glanced over at my sister as we took a walk around the lake. It was early August and too hot to do much more than walk, not that it had stopped Jewel from running ahead and promising to catch up with us on her loop back. It was never too hot for my sister-in-law to run; she actually liked it for some reason.

"My girlfriend? I guess? I mean, we haven't really talked about labels."

"How many nights have you spent together the last month?"

"Most of them."

"She's your girlfriend," Alice said decisively. "You're going to need to bring her over for dinner. I have to meet this woman."

"I don't know Alice," I hesitated. "I mean, no offense, but you can be a lot."

"Would you rather she meet Mom first?" Alice asked. "I'm sure Mom would be super interested to hear that you're spending so much time with someone. She'd probably camp out at your place until she caught you two together."

"That's low," I snapped, understanding the implied threat.

"You want me to keep my mouth shut? Bring Heidi to dinner."

"Um, how would you feel about coming to my sister's for dinner?" I asked later that night.

Heidi was wrapped around me in the big spoon position after we'd had another round of mind-blowing sex. Over the last month, we'd tried every position and made love in every room in both of our apartments and still we couldn't get enough of each other. I loved it.

Honestly, I loved her, but I wasn't quite ready to say it yet. And other than that mumbled pronouncement she'd made the first time we had sex, she hadn't said anything either. Clearly we were on the same page about taking our time.

"You want me to meet your sister?" she asked carefully.

I flopped over to face her so I could gauge her reaction.

"Yeah she's been bugging me non-stop that it's time for her to meet my girlfriend."

Heidi's face lit up, and I was once again struck by how beautiful she was. Over the last month, I'd learned she was as beautiful inside as she was on the outside. She was thoughtful, affectionate, generous, and fun to be around.

"Oh good, we're saying girlfriend now? I wasn't sure."

"Why didn't you ask?"

"I didn't want to freak you out," she explained. "But now that it's out in the open, my parents have been dying to meet you too. I was hoping we could go down to Portland for a weekend soon before my mother explodes from curiosity about you."

"Wow, okay."

We spent the next two months cycling through meeting each other's family and friends. First I introduced her to Alice and Jewel, then my daughters a few days later. I figured my sister and her wife would like Heidi, but I wasn't sure how my girls would react. To my relief, they took to Heidi right away, and by the time we'd finished dinner the three of them were ganging up on me and giving me shit about something.

After we'd passed those hurdles, I took some vacation days during the week so we could drive down to Portland. Weekends were Heidi's prime days for big tips at the restaurant, so we traveled midweek to spend two days with Heidi's parents, even sleeping in her childhood bedroom.

When I couldn't put it off any longer, I introduced Heidi to my parents. Dad was, as I expected, pretty stoic. Now that he knew that he could still have his bromance with my ex-husband Rob, he honestly didn't seem to care who I was dating.

My mother of course was another story.

After several pointed comments over dinner about divorce, abandoning people, and children from "broken homes", I'd finally snapped.

"Mom! This is my life and my business. Rob and I have been divorced for months now, so you can move on, or we can stop talking altogether, your choice!"

Mom's mouth snapped open in shock. I always went along with her not-so-passive aggression, but tonight, I'd had enough.

"And just so we're clear, I'm happier with Heidi than I ever was with Rob. I loved my ex-husband, but I'm *in* love with Heidi. Deal with it!"

Across the table, my father sucked his lips in to smother a smile.

Heidi's hand came to my thigh, and she leaned in close to whisper in my ear.

"I love you too."

I whipped my head around to meet her eyes. "You do?"

After all this time, I hadn't been sure if that comment before she fell asleep had been real or just wishful thinking.

Her smile was sweet. "Yes, of course I do."

"Let's go home."

After bidding goodbye to my parents, we headed to Heidi's apartment. When we got there, we went straight to bed, laying on the comforter fully clothed and staring into each other's eyes.

"So, dinner was fun," Heidi said.

I rolled my eyes.

"Sorry about my mother. Not to make any excuses for her, but this has been a big adjustment for her."

"Say it again," Heidi ordered.

"My mother's a loon," I joked.

Heidi raised one eyebrow, waiting.

"I love you."

"I love you too, Rebecca. So much."

I rolled on top of her, sliding my leg between hers so we could grind our pussies against each other's thighs. It was one of our favorite ways to get each other off, allowing us to be face to face when we came. Our movements were frantic, and we didn't even wait to take our clothes off, instead dry humping each other until we were both shaking with our orgasms.

After we'd found our release together, we lay there snuggling, each of us lost in our own thoughts.

"As long as we're all in love and stuff now, there's something I've been wanting to bring up."

Heidi's voice was unusually hesitant. I stiffened.

"What, honey? What's the matter?"

"Both of our apartments are too damned small."

We'd been alternating between the two homes, but we both lived in tiny studio apartments, not leaving us with a lot of space when we spent time together outside the bed.

"Yeah..."

I wasn't totally sure where she was going with this.

"My lease is coming up next month, and I was thinking maybe we'd feel more comfortable living in a larger apartment. Together."

"Are you asking me to move in with you?" I asked.

"Technically I'm asking that we move in together someplace new," she reminded me. "I've loved living alone since my divorce, but I'd love it even more if we woke up together every morning, in our own place, a place that's larger than a shoebox."

"Plus we won't be constantly looking for things we left at the other person's house," I added.

When you spent nearly every night alternating between apartments, it was easy to lose track of things.

"That too," she laughed.

"I'd love to move in together," I said.

Heidi's face lit up with pleasure. "Really?"

"We've spent nearly every day together over the past few months, seeing each other at our best and worst. We've met each other's families, and we've even farted around each other. The mystery is gone, and we are still in love. I think it's pretty obvious that we're in this for the long haul."

"There is no one else I'd rather spent the long haul with," she said.

"Me either, baby. Me either."

As I pulled Heidi closer, I sent a little prayer of gratitude that I'd listened to my sister. If I hadn't committed to going on so many first dates, I probably wouldn't have met Heidi. I fell asleep secure in the knowledge that I'd never go on a first date again.

Chapter Twenty-Five: The Happily Ever After

One year later...

"Are you sure about this honey? I've got my car keys if you want to make a run for it."

I smacked my father's arm. He looked very distinguished in his suit that he only wore for weddings and funerals.

"Dad! You said the exact same thing the first time I got married."

"I remember."

He looked down at me, his expression serious.

"You know I love Rob, but I've never seen you so happy as you've been the last year with Heidi. It's been a nice thing to see you blossom."

I reached up to give him a hug. Dad wasn't much of a talker, but when he did speak, it was always impactful.

"Thanks Dad, I am happy."

Heidi and I had been living together for about six months when we decided to tie the knot. I would have gone to the courthouse the next day, but she really wanted to finish grad school first.

Living together had been an easy adjustment. We both had our own lives, but we also spent time together, cooking dinner, going to the farmer's market, hiking, and hanging out with our ever-growing circle of friends.

Heidi had graduated with her Master of Social Work in May, and we'd settled on an October wedding. We'd planned the wedding like we'd done everything: together, and with open discussion. No sense in messing with what works.

We'd decided that since we both wanted our fathers to walk us up the aisle, we would enter from opposite sides of the ballroom where the ceremony was taking place and meet in the middle.

As the wedding march started, my father and I began walking. I kept my eyes fixed on Heidi the entire time as she and her father approached us from the other direction.

She looked breathtakingly lovely in a light pink cocktail dress and dark pink heels, her blonde hair pulled up into a twist.

I'd gone with an off-white dress that hit me at the knee and had an antique lace overlay. I'd left my hair loose but tucked a pink flower behind my ear.

We'd forgone traditional bridesmaids. To my surprise and pleasure, Heidi had suggested that we ask my two daughters to stand up for us. The girls loved Heidi and had eagerly agreed to be our witnesses. They were beaming as they waited for us in the middle of the ballroom, wearing matching green dresses.

I glanced around at our friends and family in the audience. My ex-husband gave us a thumbs up from the second row, his arm around a woman he'd been dating for about nine months now. He planned to propose to her at Christmas, and I was pretty sure she was going to say yes.

Rob and I were still the best of friends, and both of our significant others supported us in our friendship. We'd even gone on a couple of double dates with each other, although Alice and Jewel were our most frequent double date partners.

It was surprising how easily Heidi and I had folded into each other's lives. Now we were going to make it official.

"Ladies and gentlemen, welcome to the wedding of Rebecca and Heidi."

My sister beamed at us from her place on the dais. She'd been shocked when we'd asked her to officiate the wedding, not hesitating to get ordained online for the event. We figured it was only fitting since in a roundabout way she'd gotten Heidi and me together.

"Finding love at any age is a beautiful thing," Alice started. To my surprise, she was getting a little misty eyed. "It's a gift to find someone who accepts you just as you are, and is committed to bringing out their best, to meet the best in you."

Behind me, I could hear my mother sniffing loudly.

"And now Rebecca and Heidi will share their vows."

I faced the love of my life, reciting my vows by heart. I promised to love her forever, to let her control the thermostat, and that I'd finally give in to her pleas to adopt a cat. In turn, Heidi promised to love me forever, to make me breakfast every Sunday, and to stop leaving the cap off the toothpaste.

After my sister pronounced us officially married, we flew together, sealing our marriage with a kiss that earned us a round of applause. We walked back down the aisle hand in hand, ready to start our happily ever after.

***

Want to read about how Rebecca's sister Alice got together with Jewel? Check out "My BFF's Sister[1]", part of the Friends to Lovers contemporary lesbian romance series. You can find more of Reba's lesbian romances at

Books2read.com/rl/lesbianromance[2]

If you liked this book, please consider leaving a review or rating to let me know.

Be sure to join my newsletter for more great books. You'll receive a free book when you join my newsletter. Subscribers are the first to hear about all of my new releases and sales. Visit my mailing list sign-up at bit.ly/RebaBaleSapphic[3] to download your free book today.

---

1. https://books2read.com/u/4NxD1J

2. *https://books2read.com/rl/lesbianromance*

3. https://bit.ly/RebaBaleSapphic

Special Preview

The Divorcee's First Time
A Contemporary Lesbian Romance

By Reba Bale

"It's done," I said triumphantly. "My divorce is final."

My best friend Susan paused in the process of sliding into the restaurant booth, her sharply manicured eyebrows raising almost to her hairline. "Dickhead finally signed the papers?" she asked, her tone hopeful.

I nodded as Susan settled into the seat across from me. "The judge signed off on it today. Apparently his barely legal girlfriend is knocked up, and she wants to get a ring on her finger before the big event." I explained with a touch of irony in my voice. "The child bride finally got it done for me."

Susan smiled and nodded. "Well congratulations and good riddance. Let's order some wine."

We were most of the way through our second bottle when the conversation turned back to my ex. "I wonder if Dickhead and his Child Bride will last for the long haul," Susan mused.

I shook my head and blew a chunk of hair away from my mouth.

"I doubt it," I told her. "Someday she's gonna roll over and think, there's got to be something better out there than a self-absorbed man child who doesn't know a clitoris from a doorknob."

Susan laughed, sputtering her wine. I eyed her across the table. Although she was ten years older than me, we had been best friends for the last five years. We worked together at the accounting firm. She had been my trainer when I first came there, fresh out of school with my degree. We bonded over work, but soon realized that we were kindred spirits.

Susan was rapidly approaching forty but could easily pass for my age. Her hair was black and shiny, hinting at her Puerto Rican heritage, with blunt bangs and blond highlights that she paid a fortune for. Her face was clear and unlined, with large brown eyes and cheek bones that could cut glass. She was an avid runner and worked hard to maintain a slim physique since the women in her family ran towards the chunkier side.

I was almost her complete opposite. Blonde curls to her straight dark hair, blue eyes instead of brown, curvy where she was lean, introverted to her extrovert.

But somehow, we clicked. We were closer than sisters. Honestly, I don't know how I would have gotten through the last year without her. She had been the first one I called when my marriage fell apart, and she had supported me throughout the whole process.

It had been a big shock when I came home early one day and found my husband getting a blow job in the middle of our living room. It had been even more shocking when I saw the fresh young face at the other end of that blow job.

"What the fuck are you doing?" I had screeched, startling them both out of their sex stupor. "You're getting blow jobs from children now?"

The girl had looked up from her knees with eyes glowing in righteous indignation. "I'm not a child, I'm nineteen," she had informed me proudly. "I'm glad you finally found out. I give him what you don't, and he loves me."

I looked into the familiar eyes of my husband and saw the panic and confusion there. I made it easy for him. "Get out," I told him firmly, my voice leaving no room for argument. "Take your teenage girlfriend and get the fuck out. We're getting a divorce. Expect to hear from my lawyer."

The condo was in my name. I had purchased it before we were married, and since I had never added his name to the deed, he had no rights to it. There was no question he would be the one leaving.

My husband just stared at me with his jaw hanging open like he couldn't believe it. "But Jennifer," he whined. "You don't understand. Let me explain."

"There's nothing to understand," I told him sadly. "This is a deal breaker for me, and you know that as well as I do. We are done."

The girl had taken his hand and smiled triumphantly. "Come on baby," she told him. "Zip up and let's get out of here. We can finally be together like we planned."

"Yeah baby," I had sneered. "I'll box up your stuff. It'll be in the hallway tomorrow. Pick it up by six o'clock or I'm trashing it all."

After they left my first call was to the locksmith, but my second call was to Susan.

That night was the last time I had seen my husband until we had met for the court-ordered pre-divorce mediation. He spent most of that session reiterating what he had told me in numerous voice mails, emails and sessions spent yelling on the other side of my front door. He loved me. He had made a terrible mistake. He wasn't going to sign the papers. We were meant to be together. Needless to say, mediation hadn't been very successful. Fortunately, I had been careful to keep our assets separate, as if I knew that someday I would be in this situation.

Through it all, Susan had been my rock. In the end I don't think I was even that sad about the divorce, I was really angrier with myself for staying in a relationship that wasn't fulfilling with a man I didn't love anymore.

"You need to get some quality sex." Susan drew my attention back to the present. "Bang him out of your system."

"I don't know," I answered slowly. "I think I need a hiatus."

"A hiatus from what?" Susan asked with a frown. "You haven't had sex in what, eighteen months?"

I nodded. "Yeah, but I just can't take a disappointing fumble right now. I would rather have nothing than another three-pump chump."

I shook my head and continued, "I'm going to stick with my battery-operated boyfriend, he never disappoints me."

Susan smiled. "That's because you know your way around your own vajayjay."

She motioned to the waiter to bring us a third bottle of wine.

"That's why I like to date women," she continued. "We already know our way around the equipment."

I nodded thoughtfully. "You make a good point."

Susan leaned forward. "We've never talked about this," she said earnestly. "Have you ever been with a woman?"

For more of the story, check out "The Divorcee's First Time" by Reba Bale, available for immediate download[1] today.

***

Want a free book? Join my newsletter and a special gift. I'll contact you a few times a month with story updates, new releases, and special sales. Visit bit.ly/RebaBaleSapphic[2] for more information.

Other Books by Reba Bale

Check out my other books, available on most major online retailers now. Go to my webpage[3] at bit.ly/AuthorRebaBale to learn more.

Friends to Lovers Lesbian Romance Series
The Divorcee's First Time
My BFF's Sister
My Rockstar Assistant
My College Crush
My Fake Girlfriend
My Secret Crush
My Holiday Love
My Valentine's Gift
My Spring Fling
My Forbidden Love
Coming Out in Ten Dates
Worth Waiting For

Menage Romances
Pie Promises
Tornado Warning
Summer in Paradise
Life of the Mardi

Hotwife Erotic Romances
Hotwife in the Woods
Hotwife on the Beach
Hotwife Under the Tree
A Hotwife's Retreat
Hot Wife Happy Life

---

3.   https://books2read.com/ap/nB2qJv/Reba-Bale

Other Standalone Stories

Sinful Desires

Taken by Surprise

Want a free book? Just join my newsletter at bit.ly/RebaBaleSapphic[4].

---

4. https://bit.ly/RebaBaleSapphic

You'll be the first to hear about new releases, special sales, and free offers.

About the Author

Reba Bale writes erotic romance, lesbian romance, menage romance, & the spicy stories you want to read on a cold winter's night. When Reba is not writing she is reading the same naughty stories she likes to write.

You can also follow Reba on Medium[1] for free stories, bonus epilogues and more. You can also hear all about new releases and special sales by joining Reba's newsletter mailing list.[2]

---

1. https://medium.com/@authorrebabale
2. https://bit.ly/rebabooks

Don't miss out!

Visit the website below and you can sign up to receive emails whenever Reba Bale publishes a new book. There's no charge and no obligation.

https://books2read.com/r/B-A-IDTM-JIOIC

BOOKS 2 READ

Connecting independent readers to independent writers.

Did you love *Coming Out in 10 Dates*? Then you should read *My BFF's Sister*[3] by Reba Bale!

Her best friend's sister is strictly off-limits, especially when her friend has no idea that her little sister is a lesbian.

Jewel is back from a long stint in the Peace Corps and ready to start her new life back in her hometown. She's ready to come out to her family and live life without apology. A chance encounter with her sister's best friend Alice brings back memories of her childhood crush. Alice still sees her as the pesky kid sister, but Jewel is all grown up now and knows exactly how to take what she wants – and she wants Alice.

Can Jewel convince Alice to take a chance on love, even if it may destroy her longest friendship?

---

3. https://books2read.com/u/4NxD1J

4. https://books2read.com/u/4NxD1J

"My BFF's Sister" is book two in the "Friends to Lovers" romantic novella series. Each book in the series is a steamy standalone featuring an LGBTQ couple making the leap from friends to lovers. This book includes explicit sexual activity between consenting adults. It is intended for mature audiences only.